# The Seekers of the Clues

## Book One

# THE ALL SEEING EYE

CHARLES BESJAK

To my old cat, Jack

# Table of Contents

## Hunter



## Jenifer



## Jack

# THE ALL SEEING EYE

# Jack

## Burnt Pancakes

Jack was having a bad day; even before he found out he was adopted. He woke to the sound of rain drumming on his window. He slowly sat up and rubbed the sleep out of his eyes. Jack could hear the sound of his mum's footsteps downstairs. His father would already be at work by now.

Jack stumbled out of bed and walked to the window. A thick gray fog swallowed almost all of England. Anyone with any sense would be inside their house by a snug fire. But of course Jack would have to walk to school. They only had one car and his father needed it for work.

His father was the only one with a job in the family and he worked for a newspaper in Barry, England where they lived. He liked to write, but Jack's mum always pestered him about getting a real job. The newspaper business didn't pay very well, so Jack was always forced to get small jobs in town. This didn't bother him. He liked the jobs he got. Once he had even gotten a job at a book store. Jack loved books, like his father, so he read quite a lot.

But there would be no browsing for books today. The storm rolling in was starting to worry Jack. It didn't look normal.

"Up! Get up!" his mother yelled from somewhere down stairs.

"Coming," Jack yelling back.

He focused on getting on his school uniform. He glanced out the window again and could swear that the fog was getting darker. Jack didn't like it.

Five minutes later Jack tramped down the stairs into his small kitchen were his mother was flipping burnt pancakes. ("Never eat my mum's food," he thought.) He slumped down into a chair and looked about the room.

It was a small kitchen with one light that hung above the wooden table where they ate. A few windows were scattered carelessly across the four small walls that enclosed the room.

"Small," Jack thought. "Small, small, small."

Jacks very life was small. He'd never even seen anything more than the streets of Barry, England. Some of his classmates at school had been around the world: France, Spain, Scotland, Italy, Germany, and America. Jack wanted to see the world so badly it hurt.

At that moment his mother must have noticed him because she gave him a plate of the burnt pancakes she had been working on.

"Eat up," she said smiling, as if that would make the pancakes taste better.

"Pleasant day," Jack said glancing nervously out the window.

His mother's smile faded. She walked over to one of the many windows in the kitchen.

"Bad weather I suppose," she said.

Jack picked at his pancake. He looked up at his mother and for the millionth time wondered why he was so different from her. She had chocolate colored hair and brown eyes that could always seem to pull the truth out of you. Jack on the other hand was tall and lanky with dark black hair and strangest of all, electric blue eyes. They looked nothing alike. He had always wondered why he looked so different from his parents. They had explained to him many times that he got his unique features from some distant family relative. But Jack could never see how that could be possible.

"Ok," his mother said, turning her attention back to Jack. "Finish eating, you're going to be late."

Jack looked distastefully down at the charcoal colored lump on his plate. He figured he wouldn't be getting another meal for some time, so he choked it down.

Jack threw on an old rain coat, some boots that no longer fit, and grabbed his school bag. His mother looked him over.

"Perfect," she said beaming.

Jack couldn't see how a fifteen year old boy in old clothes that smelled of burnt pancakes could be perfect, but he decided it best not to argue. Instead Jack opened the door of his small house in Barry, England and plunged into the fog.

# Jack

## School Stinks

Jack stood looking up at the Barry Public Secondary School. There was that word again - small. The only way to describe the school was small. It was maybe twelve by twenty four meters and had only two rooms. One was the bathroom and the other was the school room. The school house had red painted walls that were always peeling and an old black roof.

Jack had never liked school. It got unbearably boring sometimes. Every time he tried to be a good student something happened which would make it turn out wrong. The only thing Jack had ever been good at learning were different languages. He already could speak fluently in French, Spanish, Italian, and German. Jack could also write a fair amount of Latin. The problem was there were no other people who he could speak to.

Luckily, Jack had just made it on time but was sopping wet with rain water. He slipped inside and took a seat in the back of the class. Miss Anderson, the only teacher, came in right behind Jack after he sat down.

"Ok," she said walking up to the chalk board, "Let's take out our spelling books and turn to page 205."

Jack had never been good at spelling so he knew it was going to be a long day. Reluctantly he took out his spelling book and opened it.

Jack glanced up at Miss Anderson who was writing lots of useless things on the board like: "Spelling is fun!" and "The word *Philosophical* has two p's in it."

Will Harris, a big kid who was sitting behind Jack, had ripped out a page of his spelling book and was making it into a paper airplane. Will's favorite thing to do was to rip things in half and Jack had learned the hard way to keep all of his school objects away from him.

After Spelling came Math and then Grammar. After that, Jack was so bored he fished the book he had been working on out of his desk - *Treasure Island.* He was only half way through it and couldn't put it down. Jack opened it to read under his desk.

Then just like lightning, Will grabbed the book from behind Jack. When Miss Anderson's back was turned, Will ripped half of the pages out of the book and threw them on the floor.

Jack wanted to scream, but he knew better than to tell on Will. He would just beat Jack up. Will smirked and slumped back down in his chair. Jack bit back a curse. Why couldn't he just read a simple book without getting picked on? He glared at Will and gave a simple message: "You're going to pay for that." Then he turned back around to face Miss Anderson.

After Grammar came lunch. Lunch was Jack's favorite subject. He sat as far away from Will as possible. This sadly meant he was right next to the bathroom. And the smell coming from it was disgusting. Jack was hoping his mum packed him a good lunch. Instead he got an odd sort of mangled sandwich which became his new personal low.

Jack could not stop thinking about that book he lost. The fog had cleared so he promised himself he would stop at the book store on the way home. And this time he would buy a hard cover book.

Next came Literature. The class had just finished reading the book *Swiss Family Robinson* where a family gets ship wrecked on a desert island. Jack had loved reading it, but was not so thrilled when Miss Anderson announced they would be performing a skit of the book. The point of the skit was to insure that they had read the book. Jack wasn't sure how that would help but he couldn't exactly argue. Will was to be the father, Abigail the mother, Charles the oldest son, Alfred the middle son and Arthur the youngest son. Oh, and what was Jack? He was the dog. And every time Miss Anderson would turn her back, Will would give Jack a good kick in the side. Jack's day was going great.

Finally the end of the day arrived and Jack raced outside into the fresh afternoon air. It felt good to get out of that cramped school house. Jack started his normal walk home, up Hawthorne Road to the intersection and then down St. James street to their tiny house. But this time Jack turned right onto Mary's Street and walked down a little ways to the bookstore where he had once gotten a job.

It was an old-fashioned looking store with old windows, old paint, old everything. The bell rang as Jack opened the door.

"Come in, Come in," said a deep voice from inside the shop.

A man was bustling about inside, putting books into their proper places. He was big with fat bulging from under his shirt and a kindly smile.

"Hello," Jack said "I'm looking for a book."

"Well of course you are," the man said turning to face Jack "This is a book store, is it not? How may I help you?"

"Treasure Island," Jack asked "Do you have it?"

"Well, let's see," the man said rummaging through shelves of books. "No, sorry it's not here. A lad your age took pretty much all the copies just a few minutes ago."

Jack was so angry at Will he almost marched over to his house to give him a good punch in the nose.

"That's okay," Jack said trying to keep himself calm. "I'll come back another time."

And with that Jack ran off for home.

# Jack

## Secrets are Revealed

Jack arrived at his front yard just as it was getting dark. His father's car was parked in the driveway so Jack figured he must be home. The setting sun sent ghostly shadows across the grass and the woods beyond the house.

Jack ran to the door out of breath, but stopped in his tracks for he could hear voices coming from inside.

"The boy's not ready to know Martha, he'll be crushed."

"But George, he's fifteen!"

Jack's mum and dad were obviously arguing about something important. He could hear it in their voices.

Jack crept over to the window and peered in. His parents had their backs turned to him so Jack couldn't see their faces. But he did see that his mother was holding a small grey box Jack had never seen before. From what he could see, it looked to be one of his dad's old cigar boxes. Although his dad had given up smoking long ago, Jack still remembered the boxes of cigars his dad would bring home, and the horrid smell of tobacco smoke.

"He has to know," his mother pleaded.

"Not today Martha. I'm sorry. I truly am."

Jacks father, a sturdy man, put a hand on his mother's shoulder. "A few more years. Put it back in the attic," his father said.

The attic? Jack could feel a tingling sensation inside him. He was never allowed in the attic. And what did his parent want to keep secret from him? Jack had so many questions he almost barged right in to ask them.

Jack's father turned and went into the kitchen. His mother tramped up the stairs to the second floor. And then the attic, Jack supposed.

Jack quietly slipped inside and made his way into the kitchen where his dad was making a late cup of tea.

"You're home early," Jack said.

His father almost jumped a foot in the air.

"Jack, you scared me. Don't ever do that again."

"Sorry." Jack shifted uneasily from foot to foot.

"Why don't you sit down," his father asked, "and have a cup of tea."

"Listen dad, I'm really tired. I think I'm going to get some sleep," Jack said.

His father raised an eyebrow. "I can't say I ever remember a time when you actually *wanted* to go to sleep. Perhaps once. When you were a baby, your mother – "

"Look dad, I've had a long day," Jack broke in, "I need my rest." He knew from experience never to let his dad drawl on like that. They would be up all night.

Jack's father did seem a little suspicious about it, but he let him go.

Jack crept up the stairs as quietly as possible, trying not to make a sound and went through his normal bedtime routine, all the while feeling slightly on edge.

Jack lay in bed all night, unable to sleep. He tossed and turned, trying to relax but his mind kept turning back to the conversation he had overheard. "What was in the attic? What could they possibly be trying to hide from him?" They had never kept anything from him before. Or had they? These questions kept running through Jack's mind. At last, he couldn't contain his curiosity any longer.

It was nearly daybreak. The first light was just beginning to shine faintly through his window. He slipped out of bed and out of his room on the second floor and made his way toward the small door that led to the attic eaves. You see, there are some things that are better left alone, but others need to be discovered.

Jack pushed the small door open. The attic was full of so much dust that Jack could hardly breathe. He ducked down through the low door frame and crawled back through the boxes and bins that were stacked everywhere. Jack had always been claustrophobic, and this experience didn't exactly feel comfortable.

He looked nervously around for the small box his mother had been holding. He was aware his parents were sleeping in the adjacent room, and every step he took made the floor boards creak beneath his feet. No sign of it anywhere.

Jack was about to give up and go back down stairs when he spotted it. The end of the grey box was sticking out from under a ragged quilt on top of a crate.

Jack edged his way over and pulled off the quilt. He grabbed the box and stuffed it under his nightshirt, and then crept quietly back to his room.

He sat on the edge of his bed, and shivered. He placed the box gently on his lap and slowly lifted the lid. Inside the box was a yellowed slip of paper. Jack turned it over and read:

Mount Sinai, Manhattan NY

**Certificate of Birth**

This certifies that *Jack Samuel Callow*

Was born to *Lucy and Charles Callow*

In this hospital at *3:51* o'clock, *P.M.* on *Thursday*

The *28* day of *January 1996*

Jack cradled the paper in his hands. It was his birth certificate. Jack had never seen his birth certificate.

Then a horrid thought hit him. Jack re-read the paper. Jack's parents weren't named Lucy or Charles, nor was his last name Callow. Jack's last name was Miller and he wasn't born in New York.

It was then that he realized that there were three more things in the box. One was a newspaper clipping, the other was a very old and torn book, and the other was an envelope. Jack slowly opened the envelope and found an odd looking key inside.

Jack placed the birth certificate and key gingerly on his nightstand and picked up the newspaper clipping. Jack only had time to read the headline: TERRIBLE CRASH before he turned to see his father standing in the doorway.

"You're up early," his dad offered. Then, he looked down at the paper on the table and then nervously back at Jack.

"It seems your mother was right," he said sighing, "You would eventually figure it out."

Jack was speechless. He was too stunned to do anything but just stand there and stare at his dad.

"You're... you're... not my dad," Jack stammered.

"No," his father said calmly, "I am your father."

"You're not my dad!" Jack yelled at his father.

He could feel anger and hatred bubbling up inside of him. Jack was angry at Will, himself, his mum and dad for not telling him sooner, but mostly his real parents for abandoning him.

"You never told me!" Jack screamed, "Never!"

"Jack," his father said "You need to calm down."

"No!" Jack yelled.

He pushed a pile of books that lay on his nightstand and everything crashed to the floor. The old book and the key lay unharmed on the nightstand, but the small wooden box tumbled to the floor. Jack was still holding the newspaper clipping. He was so angry he almost tore it in half.

Jack's dad put a hand on his shoulder but Jack pushed away. He turned around, grabbed the items from the box and fled down the stairs not knowing where he was going or why. But Jack had to go somewhere. He had to run away.

He met his mum on the stairs but pushed passed her and kept on running, not looking back. Leaving his mother standing there wondering what she did wrong. Jack kept on running and running, the book in one hand and the certificate, newspaper, and key in the other. He ran out the door and into the early morning air. He ran passed the driveway and his father's car. Jack ran down St. James Street and turned the corner. Onlookers watched in amazement as Jack tore down the road. He raced all the way down to the docks where he stopped, panting.

Jack didn't know what had happened back there, but one thing was for sure - he was alone and confused. He wanted to believe that it was all a dream. But Jack knew better than that. He realized that he was trembling, not from the cold but from anger and frustration.

Jack couldn't be adopted. It didn't make any sense. His life had always been good. "Okay," Jack admitted, "It had been a little rough at times." But he could still remember the happy moments he had spent with his parents. He could still remember all the times when he was younger. Jack would jump on his dad when he came back from work, and his mum would always help him with his homework. That couldn't all be fake. Could it?

There had always been that nagging thought in the back of Jack's head, Why had he looked so different from his parents? "That would explain it," Jack thought.

He blinked back tears from his eyes and paced the docks watching the ships move back and forth through the algae filled water. Jack had to be brave. He had to face the facts even if it was hard. He turned reluctantly back toward the direction of his house. He let his feet take over, for Jack knew the route home. He walked back the way he had come through the streets of Barry, England - the only place he had ever lived and known.

Jack arrived at the front of his house. The sun was now fully in the sky and Jack was momentarily blinded. His father and mother sat outside, anxiously waiting for his return. His father stood up.

"Come inside," his father said gently, "We'll have a cup of tea."

Jack walked shakily into the house with his parents. His mother and father sat at one end of the table and Jack at the other. His father handed him a cup of tea but Jack only stared at it.

"Jack you must understand that we are your parents," his father said wearily.

"NO!" Jack screamed, angrily pounding his fist on the table.

Then he realized that he was shouting and he tried to keep control of himself.

"Jack you have every right to be angry," his mother whispered, looking at him with those deep dark brown eyes.

His father pointed toward the newspaper clipping Jack was still holding.

Jack unfolded it, looked at the photo of two mangled vehicles and read the caption:

*Sunday, November 13, 1997. Terrible, head-on collision on the Long Island Expressway takes the lives of Charles and Lucy Callow, Richard Levin, and one unidentified passenger.*

"They lived in New York, in Manhattan," Jack's mother said, "It wasn't their fault. The other driver, a man, crashed into them."

Jack could feel his heart pounding.

"Why didn't you ever tell me?" Jack asked again.

"We thought that it was for the best," his father said sighing and sitting back in his chair.

"Did you ever once think of me? Ever?" he replied.

"That was all we were thinking about," Jack's mum exclaimed.

Jack gritted his teeth. He could tell she was lying.

"What is this then?" Jack asked holding up the old book.

His father bit his lip.

"This was in your parent's possession before…"

"Before it happened," Jack's mum finished.

Jack could feel tears welling up inside him but he forced himself to be strong.

"What is it?" he asked.

Jack's mother and father glanced at each other.

"A book," his father said.

Jack rolled his eyes.

"I knew that. I mean what did my mum and dad have it for?"

"We-"

"You don't know, do you?" Jack broke in.

His parents looked speechless.

Finally his mother spoke. "Open it," she said unhappily.

Jack opened the book and found himself staring at a blank page. "Nothing?" Jack asked. "There's nothing here?"

"We are sorry to say that we don't know what it means," his father said, "We kept it because it was one of the only items left in your parent's possession after the accident."

Jack tucked the book safely in his pocket along with the birth certificate and newspaper clipping. The only thing he was left holding was the key.

"I have a feeling you don't know what this is either," Jack exclaimed.

"No," his mother said.

There was an awkward pause, and then Jack's father stood up and walked over to the stove.

"How about some breakfast," he said cheerfully.

Jack didn't think that his father understood his situation because Jack did not feel like eating anything, especially if his mother was making it.

"I think that I'm going to go upstairs," Jack said shaking his head as if trying to get rid of the information he had just been told.

His mother nodded and let him go to the solitude of his room. Jack walked up the stairs in a trance, yet he had thousands of small question buzzing around in his head like a swarm of angry bees. Jacks life, which was already going downhill, had hit a speed bump.

He did the only thing that made him feel better. He wrote. Jack wrote all of his mixed up thoughts trying to organize them. But it was like trying to straighten out a tangled slinky.

If Jack couldn't trust his parents who could he trust? He sat at his desk thinking over the situation in further and further depth. He had so little information. Yes, he had names and he knew it had happened in Manhattan. But that wasn't enough for Jack. He had to know more. And his writing wasn't helping him like normal. He spent the day in contemplation, wondering whether he would ever figure out this mystery.

By evening, Jack wasn't angry at his parents anymore. He was just confused and frustrated. He didn't sleep a wink that night and in the morning he felt like a zombie. It was Saturday which meant no school and no Will. And that was good enough for Jack.

He ate breakfast in a daze and afterward stumbled out the door without a word to his parents. Jack made his way to the place he had decided on last night - the library. He had to figure out more.

Jack searched for any records of his real parents for hours. He had no luck. Once or twice Jack had to pinch himself so he wouldn't fall asleep on the news article he was reading. There were lots of interesting news articles from that date, but nothing about his parents accident. Only the New York Times piece he already had from the cigar box, and all it provided was a small caption with his parent's names, a photo of the crash scene, and that there were no survivors from a head-on collision. Now he was frustrated with himself for not finding anything that would lead him to a more complete explanation of who he is.

Jack blinked furiously as he walked out of the library, exhausted from no sleep. "Nothing," Jack thought, "nothing at all." He fidgeted nervously on his walk home. Jack's parents had given him basically nothing to work with and the same names kept on running through his head- Lucy and Charles Callow.

Jack kicked the dirt angrily. Then a crazy idea popped into his head. It was defiantly crazy, but if Jack did it, he might have a chance at finding out who he truly was. The only way to figure out more about himself, he realized, was to go to the place the incident had happened. Jack had to go to Manhattan. It was insanely crazy, but there was still a small amount of hope, and Jack couldn't ignore that.

He considered his living parents and what they would say. He didn't want to hurt them. Jack felt torn. If he stayed, he could go on having his usual life and not risk opening Pandora's Box. But then he would never know his whole story. If he went to Manhattan, maybe he could unlock the mystery of who he really is, which had always been nagging at him deep down, like there was a piece of the puzzle missing. But would he lose everything he already had? No path lead both ways.

# Jack

## The Cargo Ship

It was getting dark. Jack paced his room packing and unpacking his school bag not sure what to do. He could hear his parents down stairs. If only they knew what he was about to do.

After a good amount of thought, Jack came up with a plan. It was simple and easy if done right. He would secretly board a cargo ship heading to America. Once there, he would make his way to Manhattan. The only problem was - Jack didn't know how he was going to board the ship unseen. And if he was seen, well, that wouldn't be good.

Jack sat down on his bed, feeling torn about leaving his home. He reached into his bag and pulled out the old book that had belonged to the parents he had never known. He began to flip through the few yellowed pages that remained in the book. Jack had noticed earlier that some of the pages that had once been in the book had been torn from the binding. Suddenly, he froze. Something had caught his eye at the back of the book. He stared down at a handwritten page. Jack couldn't make out any words or anything recognizable in the writing. He skimmed his hand across the page. It was a series of marks that seemed to be a code or maybe even a language of some kind. Jack examined the marks for some time, until he became frustrated. Jack had never come across any language he could not understand.

"That confirms it," thought Jack. He was determined to leave for America. He just had to figure out what these marks meant.

Jack slung his bag over his shoulder and waited for his parents to go to sleep. He counted his breaths but lost count at about 109. He waited and waited. Finally Jack heard footsteps on the stair. He crouched down and could see shadows from under the door. Jack figured it had probably been about an hour, which would make it 11:30 pm. He heard the sound of running water and then the lights flickered off. The only sound that could be heard was the sound of Jacks heart beating.

He stood up cautiously and walked over to the door. He pushed it open and stepped down the stairs, trying desperately to stop the floorboards from creaking. Jack made his way to the tiny kitchen where he had once sat happily with his parents. "It feels funny to be leaving this place," Jack thought.

He stepped into the living room and saw all of the old pictures of himself and his parents. Jack couldn't do this, it was bloody crazy! But then again, he might not get another chance. He closed his eyes and opened the last remaining door that lead into the outside world - the place he had always wanted to see his entire life. Now, Jack wasn't so sure. It took all his will power to focus on the task ahead. A tiny voice inside of him said "Don't go, don't go." but Jack ignored it and slipped into the darkness.

The blackness swallowed him. Jack could barely see anything at all. How could he have been so stupid as to not have brought his torch? He fumbled around for any means of light. He managed to grab some matches out of his bag. Jack lit one and held it up to see with, but instantly the cold night wind blew it out. He cursed under his breath. He stared out into the night and walked toward the road. The faint light from several lamp posts lit his way. It took him maybe twenty minutes to get down to the docks.

Jack remembered that he had stood here not one day ago wondering who he was. That question was still a mystery to Jack but he intended to find the answer. He wrapped his sweater tighter around him. The wind coming off the ocean was bitter cold and Jack hoped he wouldn't have to swim to Manhattan.

Then all of a sudden, he heard voices coming from in front him. At first Jack wasn't sure if he had just been imagining things, but the voices were getting steadily louder. He ducked under some big crates of cargo that were waiting to be loaded. Two men appeared from behind a docked ship.

"James you fool! I told you this was the wrong ship."

"But Adam," came a deep voice.

"Listen, you idiot!"

There was a loud thud and then the man whose name must have been James grunted.

"Ouch, Adam that hurt," said James.

"Just shut up and listen to me! This ship is leaving for America in half an hour – it's the wrong ship moron! Just keep moving or I'll have to slap you again."

"I got it Adam, I got it Adam," James broke in.

"Grrrr! can you please stop using my name after every word you say!"

"Okay Adam, I got it."

"I thought I told you to... Never mind. We need to get to the right ship, get the crates off, and get outta here!"

"Yes Adam, Yes," said James.

Both men walked off, Adam shouting at James all the while. Jack didn't know what they had been talking about but one thing was for sure - the ship in front of Jack was leaving for America in thirty minutes. He had to get on it. It was now or never. No turning back. But the question was - how was he going to get on? He couldn't possibly just walk right through the main entrance without being spotted. He noticed several guards and what looked to be security cameras.

Then Jack had another one of his crazy ideas. His first crazy idea had gotten him this far, so Jack decided to trust this one too. He had to hide inside one of the crates that were being loaded onto the ship. Yes, definitely insane.

Jack made his way over to the loading dock near the ship. He hid behind the huge metal crates and coils of rope to avoid detection. It was pure luck that Jack even made it half way. Once or twice a guard almost saw him.

Jack looked around and saw an open crate. It looked like they were still in the process of loading it with something. Jack darted over to the crate, and slipped inside. It was dark and cold, but there was plenty of room. He hoped they wouldn't be filling it with any more freight. As his eyes adjusted to the darkness, Jack could see that the crate was filled with various pieces of furniture. There were dressers, dining tables, china cabinets and other pieces of wooden furniture, all wrapped in large sheets of plastic.

Jack scouted around the crate and found a secure place to hide in the rear of the crate between two wooden tables. He ripped the plastic covering off the tables and laid them on the floor to create a makeshift bed. Once he had his area prepared, he took out his knife and walked over to the opening of the crate. Jack hoped that by jamming his knife into the metal runner of the door, he would be able to stop the doors from completely closing. Then, when the ship's crew closed the doors, the gap would provide a way for him to pry the doors open and escape for air once the crate was on-board. Just then, as if on cue some members of the ship crew came into view.

"This is the last one. Let's get it closed and on board," a man said.

Jack jumped back into the crate and to his hiding spot. The men walked over to the crate and began to close the doors. Jack prayed that his knife would hold out until he was on board. The door was closed and blackness enclosed him.

Jack heard the crane whirring outside of his box. "This is it," he thought. "I'm actually leaving."

The arm grabbed hold of Jack's crate with tremendous force and it went up, and up, and up. Then it swayed violently sideways and dropped. Jack felt his stomach come up into his throat. He had never liked rollercoaster's and the sensation of dropping didn't agree with him.

The box suddenly stopped dropping and landed lightly on the cargo deck of the ship. Jack's head was spinning. He faltered over to the door where he had jammed his knife. It was still stuck inside of the runner. Jack was so pleased with himself that he almost forgot about how tired he was. The door swung easily open. Jack had gotten himself a free ride to America.

# Jack

## An Unexpected Friend

The first thing that Jack did once on the ship was sleep. The moment he knew that he was safely secured he passed out on the bed. Jack had dreams that he was rocking back and forth on some sort of crane arm.

His deep sleep didn't last long. Jack woke to find that he was not on a crane arm but on a ship heading for America. He could tell that it was still night time because the tiny opening in the door had no light coming through it.

Jack sat up groggily rubbing his back from sleeping on hard metal. He looked at his watch, and then did a double take. That couldn't possibly be right. It read: 1:00 A.M. Jack had slept through an entire day! He stood up and stretched. "What a night," he thought. Jack felt great, like he could run a marathon.

The next thing Jack did was to eat some canned fruits that he had swiped from his kitchen before he left. After he was filled to the brim with food, he walked over to the door and slowly swung it open hoping no one would see him. The night air felt good and refreshing on Jack's face.

Everything was going as planned. "Plan," Jack thought. "I need a plan for when I get to Manhattan." He had almost forgotten the reason he had come. Jack focused on the task ahead. He sat on his temporary bed and made a list of what he was going to do. First Jack would have to find a way to Manhattan; after all, he only knew that this ship was headed for America, but not *where* in America. For all he knew, Jack could end up in Florida. Once he got to Manhattan he would find the exact street where the car crash had happened. Jack would look in libraries and anywhere else that might give him a clue to his real identity. Finally, once Jack had all of the information, he would simply organize it from start to finish, just the way he liked to organize his thoughts.

Jack felt like the king of the seas, the ruler of the ocean on a voyage to a new land, and possibly a new life. Nothing could defeat him, not even... not even... not even - sea sickness.

Two hours later, Jack was rushing constantly to the crack in the door. He was green in the face and felt awful. He had no idea how people could stand sailing. "This is the most awful thing in the world," Jack thought to himself as he fell over on his hands and knees vomiting. One thing was for sure, Jack was never going to go on another ship for the rest of his life! If this is what the real world felt like, he was scared to see or feel more of it.

"This is not going as planned," he said aloud.

Jack spent the next few days getting his sea legs. He stayed mostly inside the crate, without daring to peek out and risk being caught. He slept restlessly, ate most of the supplies he had brought with him, and spent his time planning out how he would proceed once he arrived in America. Many hours he spent simply fingering the only clues he had to go on – the birth certificate, the book and the odd key. The key in particular seemed like it held some important secret. "What could it be for?" Jack thought, "His parent's apartment?" The envelope that held it read simply 92 Delancey Street New York, NY. The key itself just had the number 73 etched into the bronze metal. How was he going to know what it went to?

Jack also spent time examining the markings at the back of the book. He was still stumped. They didn't look like numbers. Yet they weren't letters either. Jack ran through all the languages he had learned. Well, they weren't Greek or Arabic, that was for sure. And they definitely didn't resemble cuneiform or any form or hieroglyphics. He promised himself he would solve this one way or another.

On the sixth day of the voyage, something caught Jack's eye as he was sitting and writing in his journal. A shadow moved in the dim light. It darted to one side and then vanished behind a crate. He blinked, thinking he was hallucinating, but the shadow moved again. Jack crawled over to the door and peered out. There it was. The shadow was visible from behind another crate.

The first thing that came to Jack's mind was Adam and James. They might have seen Jack and gotten on the ship. But that was impossible. No one else could have gotten on. Or could they? There weren't any other open crates but the one Jack had gotten into. Could they have snuck passed the guards, and what about those security cameras? None of that seemed possible.

But yet there was someone or something out there, and Jack had the suspicion that the someone or something was watching him. He felt like a victim of one of those creepy horror films.

"Um… hello," Jack asked into the darkness, "Anyone there?"

No answer. The shadow was gone. Jack hadn't felt seasick for several days, but now he was beginning to feel very, very uneasy. He kept looking behind him to the crack in the door. Someone was definitely watching him.  Not in a bad way, just waiting. Waiting to see what Jack would do next.

A few more hours passed and the sun sent light streaming through the open door. Jack knew that the crew would be getting up soon and they would notice his crate was open. He walked over to the door to close it when he saw it again - the shadow.

"That's it," Jack shouted to nothingness, "show yourself!"

The shadow moved toward Jack from behind a crate. His heart pounded against his chest. Then a figure emerged. The figure of a boy.

# Hunter

## The Sea Voyage

Hunter wasn't very happy about climbing into the scary dark crate with a boy he didn't know, but the crew was up, and they threatened to see him. So he clambered inside.

Hunter was surprised to find that the place was actually very snug, except for the fact that it smelled like vomit. It reminded him of one of those old English houses you might see. Of course Hunter had never actually been to England. He had seen England from the boat docks, but didn't dare step foot on land.

The other boy closed the door behind him and carefully lit a candle. The light danced across the walls of the crate creating intricate golden shapes on the floor.

The boy turned so Hunter could see his face. He had black hair and electric blue eyes. "Well, that's unusual," Hunter thought to himself.

"So, who exactly are you?" he whispered, trying to keep his voice low.

"No, you got it backwards," the boy said sternly, "Who are you?"

Hunter hesitated for a moment not sure what to say.

"Hunter Truman," he offered.

The boy narrowed his eyes.

"Why were you spying on me?"

"I... I wasn't really... I just didn't know what you were doing on this ship," Hunter finished weakly.

The boy looked him over and then to Hunter's astonishment he smiled.

"Nice to meet you Hunter Truman," he said, "I'm Jack..." His smile wavered, "Jack Miller."

Jack didn't seem too sure about his name, but Hunter wasn't worried.

"Why don't you come and sit down," Jack said, "you look pretty tired."

Hunter had to admit he was exhausted. He had been sneaking around the ship for days, dodging guards, and trying to find a safe place to sleep for the night. He hadn't found one, until he had seen Jack's open crate and... well you get the idea. Hunter had never intended to spy on anyone.

"Sure, thanks," he said gratefully.

Hunter walked with Jack over to a small place between two tables. A few pieces of plastic wrap had been laid on the floor to create a sleeping space. He was amazed that anyone could have gotten on this ship. Hunter had been the only stowaway from Spain to England.

Jack pointed to a spot on the floor. Once they were settled Jack looked straight into Hunters eyes. "So, how did you get on this ship, really?"

Hunter looked down at the floor and tried to process his thoughts. "I'm here from France," he replied.

Jack's bit his lip. "France? You mean this ship stopped in France?"

"Well no… it stopped in Spain," Hunter said, a little confused. "I'm from France. It made a stop in England and we should be in America in a few days."

Jack's eyes lit up. "You mean you're from France?" he asked.

Hunter studied Jack. "Yes, I'm from France."

Jack smiled even wider. Then Jack spoke. Not in English but in perfect French. "Parle vous francais?" he asked.

Hunter cracked a smile. "Oui, Je parl francais," he replied back in French.

From that moment on the conversation was spoken in French. And after a while Hunter found it got a lot easier to talk to Jack.

Hunter told Jack that he lived in France but was originally from America. His dad had gotten a job transfer so his family had had to move. He had never liked his life in France. That's why Hunter was here - to go back to America. Of course that wasn't the main reason that Hunter was going, but he didn't tell Jack that. It was too painful to even think about.

Jack gave Hunter the whole story from his day at school to being a stowaway on this ship. They seemed to have a lot in common. Jack also explained that he had run away because of his parents. They had supposedly been very mean to him. Hunter didn't see how that could be the case, but he decided not to press him. He had not given Jack his whole story either.

"You hungry?" Jack asked, "I think I still have some left over fruit."

"Yeah," Hunter said, "Totally."

Jack looked at him, amused. "Totally?" he asked. "You talk weird."

Hunter smiled. "Thank you very much; I'm proud of my way of talking."

Jack laughed. "Come on Hunter Truman, let's have something to eat. Like you said, we'll be in America before we know it."

# Hunter

## Winter Wonderland

Land! Land! I see it. America!" Jack yelled from the door of the crate.

"Where?" Hunter asked as he slipped around a table to see.

"There!" Jack yelled.

"Shhh!" Hunter said, "You'll get us spotted."

"Oh, right," Jack said, getting control of himself.

The last couple of hours there had been a few guards lurking around the crate. Hunter decided that it must have been the smell of their food that had given them away.

"If we just make it there without those guards spotting us-"

"I know, I know," Hunter said, "we've gone over the plan at least twenty times."

"Right" Jack said, "All we have to do is not be seen, and wait until our crate is lifted on to the docks."

"And then get off when no one's around," Hunter finished.

"The only problem is, we don't know where this ship is going to land," Jack said scratching his head.

"Well, like I said before, I'm going to Chicago," Hunter exclaimed, "That's where me and my family used to live."

"Well maybe we'll be lucky and this ship will land there," Jack said hopefully.

Hunter stared at him in disbelief.

"Dude seriously, did you ever learn geography?"

"Um… no not really," Jack admitted.

He smiled. "Let's do this man."

Hunter thought they worked well together, although Jack was pretty loud. Hunter had always been small and quick for his age. That's how he had gotten on the ship; he had simply dodged the security cameras and snuck passed the guards. Hunter didn't want to admit this to Jack. He figured he'd probably look like a showoff.

Jack tripped over a table.

"Shhh! Be quieter," Hunter scolded.

"I'm sorry. I'm trying," Jack protested.

They waited and waited for a long time until finally the ship stopped at a dock. Hunter waited in pitch blackness.

"Should we open the door?" Jack asked from the darkness.

"No, we have to wait until we get loaded onto the docks."

"It's been thirty minutes."

"Trust me, not yet," Hunter said.

Thirty more minutes passed.

"Hunter, I think we should at least check," Jack whispered.

"Fine, open the door, very slowly," Hunter said.

Jack slipped open the door. Hunter blinked as the light met his eyes. And that's when everything went wrong.

There was a call from outside the crate.

"I told you I heard something! Get those kids!"

Hunter cursed as five security guards ran toward them.

"Jack, what now?"

Jack clenched his jaw. "Run! Now. Go!"

Hunter didn't need to be told twice. He was off and Jack was right behind him. The guards shouted orders into walkie-talkies and more guards showed up. They were cornered, and there was nothing they could do about it. Suddenly, Hunter had an idea. A stupid idea that would probably get them killed, but hey, what the heck.

"Jack, climb," Hunter screamed, and ran for a pile of stacked up crates.

Jack got the message. They climbed like there was no tomorrow, using the metal bars on the side of the crate like a ladder. It was probably hopeless, Hunter thought, unless they could get to the side of the ship. They could get onto the dock and then they would be on land. Jack and Hunter jumped off the last crate on the other side and hit the deck running. Crew members shouted and jumped out of the way. The dock was coming up fast.

"Almost there," Jack panted.

The guards were gaining. It took all of Hunters effort to make one last flying leap onto the docks. His eyesight went blurry and every muscle in his body screamed with pain.

Then Hunter caught a glimpse of the landscape and stopped to stare. Everything was covered in deep snow. And only then did it occur to him that it was actually snowing.

"Where are we?" Hunter said aloud.

Jack had stopped too. "This doesn't look like Manhattan."

"Tell me about it," Hunter said.

"Hey, you kids get back here!" one of the guards yelled.

"Go, go!" Hunter said, pushing Jack forward.

They ran on. Hunter noticed that there were small cottages nestled in the snow drifts and a forest beyond that. Jack veered right and Hunter followed. He was heading for the snow drifts. Then all of a sudden a voice called out from behind them. "In here, hurry!"

Hunter thought it must be a guard but that didn't make sense.

"In here, now!" the voice said again, more urgently.

It was then that Hunter realized it was coming from one of the cottages. A man, maybe in his twenties, stood at the door of the smallest of them. He had long blonde hair and dark green eyes that glittered with intelligence. His face must have been handsome at one time, but now it was ripped and torn with scars.

"In here," he said again.

Hunter looked at Jack. The man made frantic gestures for them to hurry. Jack was the first one into the house. Just like the outside, the inside was small.

"Down under the table," the man said.

Hunter and Jack crouched down under the big wooden table in the corner of the room.

"Wait here," the man said sternly.

Jack mouthed "Are you okay?"

Hunter gave him the thumbs up sign. The man opened the door to check that they were alone. The guards ran right passed the cottage.

Jack sighed. "Thank you so much," he said to the man.

The man looked both boys over distastefully. "What type of cloths are you wearing?"

"Um, jeans and a t-shirt," Hunter said hesitantly.

Then the man laughed so loud Hunter thought that the whole cottage was going to fall apart. It wasn't a kind laugh though. It was a cruel laugh. And for a moment Hunter thought that he saw the man's eyes glow. But then that moment passed, and Hunter wasn't sure if he had imagined the greedy fire in his eyes.

"You can't wear those clothes in this weather. It's below zero outside!"

Hunter and Jack exchanged nervous looks.

"I don't mean to be rude or anything but where exactly are we?" Jack asked.

"Well you're in Nova Scotia of course!"

"Nova Scotia?" Jack said in a weak voice.

"Yep, Nova Scotia," the man said proudly, "One defends and the other conquers."

"Excuse me?" Hunter asked, stunned.

"Well, it's the motto," the man said, offended.

"Oh, sorry-"

"Come on in and we'll get you some suitable clothes," the man interrupted. "Oh, and I'm Ross. Ross Voler." And with that, he walked into another small room off of the one he had been standing in.

"Ross Voler?" Hunter said once they were alone, "What kind of name is that?"

"I think its Latin," Jack exclaimed.

"What kind of person has a Latin name? And isn't Latin like a dead language or something?"

"Well yes, and no," Jack said.

"Well that clears everything up," Hunter grumbled.

"No one speaks Latin anymore but you can write it and most of the words in the English language are derived from it," Jack explained.

"That is very confusing."

Jack shook his head. "Never mind, we better follow him."

Hunter ducked under the low door frame into the other room. It was even smaller than the first and could hardly fit all three of them.

"There's a trunk over there with some warm clothes in it." Ross said. "They might be a little big but they should do."

Hunter opened the trunk and found himself looking at a life time supply of animal pelts and fur coats.

"Whoa, dude how many coats do you have?" he asked.

"Twenty seven," Ross said proudly, "All mine. Each and every one."

Jack and Hunter put on the fur coats gratefully.

"Thanks again," Jack said to Ross.

"No thanks necessary," Ross said waving his hand, "But I would like to know something. Why were you running from those guards and where did they come from?"

"Um, well…" Jack stammered, "It's sort of a long story."

Hunter nodded. "Yeah, a really long story involving flying crates, chases and multiple incidents with vomit."

Jack shot him a look that said something like "Shut up now, we can't trust him."

Hunter could understand Jack's way of thinking. Staying in this little cottage in the middle of Nova Scotia with a man whose eyes glowed wouldn't have been his first choice either.

Ross nodded unconvinced. "Well, can you at least tell me why you're here in the first place?"

"Well-" Hunter began.

"We were traveling with our parents to Manhattan when we got off at the wrong stop," Jack lied, "This is my friend, um… Will Harris, and I'm John Callow."

Hunter raised his eyebrows at Jack, but found it very hard to not burst out laughing at the same time. Of course he had to admit that Jack was a pretty quick thinker. Where had he come up with the name Will Harris?

Ross nodded again, this time slightly more convinced. He sat down in a chair and folded his arms in his lap. "I recognize your English accent," Ross exclaimed, pointing to Jack.

Jack shifted from foot to foot. "Yes," he said, "I'm from England."

"Then what are you doing traveling to Manhattan with your… parents?" Ross pressed on.

The room fell silent. Nothing could be heard but the sound of snow whistling through the wind outside the door. Hunter wanted to help Jack but he didn't know what to say, and he couldn't take the risk of telling too much to Ross. Yes he had probably saved their lives and he had given them warm clothes. But the whole thing with Ross's eyes glowing brought back bad memories. The memories Hunter had been running from his entire life - memories that brought back so much pain and suffering.

He could remember the times he had sat up in his room wondering if his sister would ever get better. None of that had been happy. Hunter could also remember the time when he was nine; the day his sister went outside for the first time in their new home in France. She had seen a child get run over by a car.

Mary had always been unrealistically scared over the smallest things, but this particular incident triggered everything to go wrong. She had never been the same after that. She would never go outside again, but would sit in the corner of the dark basement. Mary would tell everyone that came near that she would get run over by a car if she went outside. Her problems only got worse and she wouldn't come out of the basement for days on end.

Hunter and his parents had tried to talk to her, to make her come out, but she would never listen. Finally Hunter couldn't take it anymore. He wanted to help so badly, but everything he tried failed. So he ran away, heading for Chicago - his old home. Hunter could never go back. He needed to have some time to think things over.

"Well then," Ross said, bringing Hunter back to the present, "I suppose I'll have to let you sleep here for the night. In the mean time I'll call your parents. Do you have their number?"

"No," Jack said quickly, "I don't think I have it on me."

"Me neither," Hunter said, "but I think I might still have that Hershey bar somewhere."

Apparently that comment didn't help because Jack gave him another one of those "Shut up now!" looks.

"Look, we're really tired. Can we please sleep here for the night and maybe tomorrow, after me and um... Will sort out, you know... stuff, we can call our parents," Jack asked.

Ross eyed them. "Very well," he said nodding his head. "But understand one thing. If you intend to steal anything-"

Hunter and Jack shook their heads in unison, with lots of "No's," and "We'd never do anything like that."

Ross pointed to the room they had just come from. "There is a bed to your left."

Hunter was happy to get out of that room, but apparently Jack's bag wasn't. It got caught on the corner of a bookshelf and its contents spilled out onto the floor. Jack rushed around picking up various items. Hunter knelt down to help, but something wasn't right. Ross had that look in his eye again but this time he was looking at something on the floor; a very old very torn book that had fallen from Jack's bag.

Then multiple things happened at once. Ross lunged for the book. Jack realizing what was going on, jumped in the way and intercepted Ross's hand, and Hunter (the innocent bystander) leapt back in surprise. This nice conversation had just turned into a wrestling match between Jack and Ross.

"That book!" Ross yelled, "Where did you find that book!"

Jack's face was white with fear. "I don't know, it was my parents."

Ross jumped to his feet and stood there dumfounded staring from Jack to the book and back again.

"You're... you're parents," he stammered.

"My parents are dead now but it used to be theirs."

"Aha!" Ross said, "I knew you were lying. Once I return that book to headquarters...Yes, yes, yes!" Ross turned his attention back to Jack. "You don't know who you are boy, do you? Give me the book and you can go free. You can go at peace. If you give me the book all will be well... Yes, yes, all will be well!" he said insanely.

Silence filled the room.

"Dude," Hunter said, "way too much caffeine."

Ross's facial features suddenly got all distorted. His glittering eyes were too bright to look at. Ross had the look of a man who was mad, knew he was mad, and was happy about it.

If possible, Jack's face turned even paler.

"Uh, Jack," Hunter said surprised at how calm his voice sounded, "Don't you think we should get back to our parents?"

"Oh, and your name isn't John either is it boy?" Ross said, stumbling forward and grabbling Jack by the shirt collar, "Give me that book!!"
Then Jack did something that really surprised Hunter. He shoved Ross off of himself and to the floor. Ross hit the table they had hid under and went spinning off somewhere to the right. Hunter looked at Jack.

"What now?" he said.

Jack pulled some rope out of his bag. "Crazy idea time.  Quick, get out and help me secure the door!"

# Hunter

## Camping in Nova Scotia Isn't Fun

Hunter and Jack wrapped the rope around the door. Screams could be heard from inside. Ross obviously did not want to play peak-a-boo. Hunter didn't know what had happened in there, but his main goal right now was to not be trampled by Mr. Evil Glowing Eyes.

As soon as the door was shut tight, both boys ran for the woods. It seemed to be the only shelter they could think of because Hunter was not staying in any more of those huts. Once they reached the dense thicket of trees, Hunter stopped to catch his breath.

"I think... I think we lost him," he panted.

Jack rounded on Hunter. "Maybe a little help next time," he said glaring at him.

"Ok," Hunter said holding his hands up in surrender, "I was under pressure. What was that all about any way?" Hunter looked down at the old book Jack was holding. "You said that your parents were dead back there, but you told me–"

"I don't care what I told you!" Jack shouted at Hunter shoving the book into his bag.

Hunter looked down at the ground. "Sorry it's none of my business." Hunter didn't know what to say. Jack looked away from him and there was a long awkward pause. "I guess I owe you one for back there," Hunter said, "I was being stupid."

Jack closed his eyes for a moment and then reopened them looking at Hunter. He nodded slowly and slung his ripped bag over his shoulder. "Come on, that rope won't hold back Ross for long, and we need to find a place to sleep for the night." He turned around and trudged off into the woods.

Every time something good would happen in Hunters miserable life he always seemed to do something idiotic that would crush his small ray of light. But this time Hunter was sure he had really done it.

He walked through the woods feeling worse than he ever had in his life. Why had Hunter said those things back there? He realized now that it wasn't a joke. That was Hunter - the big joker. The big joker who always got himself into trouble when he was just trying to have fun. And whenever he tried to be serious he ended up getting in trouble anyway.

Jack walked ahead in silence. Then suddenly he stopped, and Hunter who wasn't paying attention ran right into the back of him. They were deep in the woods now. Hunter rubbed his head.

"Here's good," Jack said, "Now, help me set up camp."

"Camp?"

Jack reached for his bag and pulled out a folded up, miniature tent.

"Wow! Dude, no way," Hunter said grinning, "Where'd that come from?"

"It's my dad's. Help me set it up."

Hunter was really confused. First Jack had parents, then he didn't, then he did again. So he did as he was told and didn't argue about it, hoping Jack would give him some clue as to what was going on. But just as Hunter suspected, Jack said nothing. And Hunter said nothing either. They worked in silence.

The sun had set and there was only one thing Hunter could think about right now and that was sleep. Thankfully the tent was cramped, but could fit two.

By the time they settled in, Jack wasn't as mad at Hunter anymore which came as a relief. Although he did still feel bad about the whole thing.

Jack was the first to speak. "Look Hunter, I may have said some things back there that were kind of, you know, mean."

This came as a complete shock. Hunter had expected Jack to say something more along the lines of: "Hunter you're so annoying," or "Hunter you stink." But Jack was actually apologizing.

"No," Hunter said, "It was my fault. I wasn't thinking."

Jack looked him straight in the eye. "I'm traveling to Manhattan, but I don't know how to get there. You can help me. Hunter please, I need you."

This was even more shocking. "Hunter I need you?" That was new.

"But Jack, I need to get to Chicago."

"Why?" Jack asked.

"It's… it's complicated."

Jack stared off into the blackness. "This book obviously means something. Otherwise Ross wouldn't want it so badly."

Hunter wasn't sure if Jack even realized he was still there, he seemed so deep in thought. "Where did you find it," Hunter asked tentatively.

Jack looked back at Hunter. Those electric blue eyes seemed to be looking right into his soul.

"It's complicated," Jack challenged.

Hunter sighed. "Well I guess you deserve the whole truth."

Jack waited patiently.

Hunter told Jack everything he had to tell. Most of it was blurred syllables. Hunter had never told anyone his real story before.

"What happened to your sister," Jack asked, "After you left. Do you know?"

"No," Hunter said trying to keep it together.

"Did you ever find out what was wrong with her?"

Hunter blinked back tears. "No," he said again, "All we knew was that her previous family had a history of mental problems. We adopted her when she was a baby."

Jack flinched at the word adopted. And at that flinch, Hunter realized exactly what was going on. It explained everything, and all at once Hunter felt a sense of guilt. He had had no idea what Jack was going through.

"I suppose I better tell you my whole story as well," Jack said.

"There's no need," Hunter exclaimed, "I understand."

Jack closed his eyes.

"What happened to them?" Hunter asked.

"They died in a car crash," Jack said miserably.

"I'm so sorry," Hunter said, "They used to live in Manhattan, right?"

Jack nodded.

"I found this book in my attic. It was in a box with my birth certificate and a newspaper clipping about the crash."

"What is it?" Hunter asked, concerned.

"I have no idea," Jack said, "But one thing is for sure. I need to get to Manhattan. You've lived on this continent before, what do I do? Where do I go?"

Hunter thought about his life. He hardly knew what he was doing anymore. Nothing seemed to make sense. Hunter just had one thought on his mind and that was getting to Chicago.

Jack seemed so helpless, and he was actually asking for Hunter's help. He'd never gotten an offer like this before. There was no way he could turn it down.

"All right," Hunter said, "I'll help you under one condition."

"And what's that?" Jack asked.

"If we meet anyone with green eyes again, *we stay away*." Hunter put emphasis on the last three words.

Jack smiled. "Deal."

"Now go to sleep," Hunter exclaimed in French, "Like you said, we'll be in America before we know it."

# Hunter

## Dan's the Man

Hunter awoke to the sound of the wind blowing outside the tent. It was bitter cold and he had to say he was happy for the fur coat. Hunter stepped outside into the early morning air. Jack stood at the edge of the clearing making something that looked like a camp fire. He was lighting match after match with no success. Every time he lit one the cold wind blew it out. Hunter walked over to him.

"Morning," he said yawning, "Beautiful day."

Jack looked up from what he was doing. "You don't have any money do you; I think these matches are almost gone."

"That I can help you with," Hunter said pulling out his wallet. "I've got, um… exactly thirty three cents."

Jack rolled his eyes. "I meant Canadian money. I've got thirty-nine pounds on me at the moment," Jack added. "We need to get something to eat before we plan."

"Plan for what?" Hunter asked.

"How we're going to get to America, duh!"

"Oh, right," Hunter said, "You do have a plan, right?"

"I probably could think of one if I had a map."

"I've got a map of Italy, but I don't think that's going to help us."

"So, we don't have a map, and we have no idea what type of transportation system we're going to use to get to Manhattan," Jack said frustrated.

"Well let's take it one step at a time," Hunter said, "First we have to get out of these woods."

Ten minutes later Jack and Hunter were stumbling through the woods with no idea where they were headed. Hunter half expected Ross to jump out of nowhere and ambush them, because last night he had thought that he'd heard something outside their tent. Hunter put that thought out of his mind and tried to concentrate on keeping up with Jack.

After about an hour of trudging through snow and tripping over hidden roots, both boys stepped out into the open. They were on the top of a hill and Hunter could see more small cottages below them, but these were slightly bigger.

A rusty water tower read: Welcome to Sambro, Nova Scotia.

"Well, at least we know where we are," Hunter exclaimed, "Let's go down there and ask somebody for help."

He knew Jack didn't like the idea, but it was their only choice. They tramped down the hill and found themselves in the middle of a small town. It looked to be basically one main street with a few stores. Off to the left Hunter saw a church and at that very moment Jack exclaimed, "Perfect, a church. Let's go there and get warm until we can figure out what to do."

Both boys headed to the church and discovered that not only was it a church but a shelter as well that served food to the homeless. They got soup and sandwiches and sat down at a table in the corner of the small cafeteria.

After a few minutes of discussion that was going nowhere as far as getting to Manhattan, the man who had served the boys lunch approached their table. He was older and had been very kind to the boys when he greeted them at the church, inviting them in for lunch.

"So boys, is the hot lunch warming you up? My name's Dan. Mind if I sit down a bit?"

Hunter and Jack both nodded, hesitantly.

Dan pulled up a chair and sat down easily. "So where are you headed? Are you camping nearby?"

Jack was the first one to speak. "We camped nearby last night" was all Jack would offer.

Dan nodded, and sat back comfortably in his chair. "It's beautiful camping country out here, that's for sure. You know, I've come out here for the past forty years. The first few years I just packed a tent and some camping supplies. I came to love it so much that I eventually bought a small cottage and now I spend half my year here. Just fishing and hunting and enjoying the beauty of nature. When I'm not working here in the shelter of course."

"So where do you live the other half of the year?" Hunter asked curiously.

"Well, I'm from Florida originally. Born and raised in Tallahassee. Most of my family still lives down there. They think I'm nuts spending half my life living way up here in the wilderness, but I wouldn't have it any other way," he replied. "Where you boys from?"

"England," Jack blurted just as Hunter said, "France." They both looked at each other. Jack kicked Hunter in the shin.

"We're both from England," Jack said, as Hunter winced in pain.

"Well ya don't say," Dan said smiling, "Never been to England. I hear it's a wonderful place. The only travel I do is back and forth from Florida to Nova

Scotia. Long trip. In fact, I'm just headed home to start packing up and closing up my cottage here for the winter. I'm heading down to Florida as soon as I can get all my belongings squared away. I like nature, but not when it's twenty below!"

Hunter felt a spark of excitement.

"Really?" Jack asked quickly, "We're heading out of here too. Down to Manhattan. Well, at least we're hoping to. But we don't quite have the transportation part worked out yet ..." Jack trailed off.

"Actually," Hunter said, "That's what we were just discussing."

"Interesting," Dan said, smiling. "Now that's quite a coincidence" he added, amused.

"Would you know of any rental car places or um... bus stations or anything like that nearby?" Hunter stammered.

"Not exactly. But if you boys would be willing to come by tomorrow and do some work around my cottage to help me get ready for my trip, I'd be willing to give you a lift down to New York state. Kind of a barter, where you could earn your transportation," Dan explained.

Hunter felt so happy he could have jumped up and hugged the guy. But instead he just answered, "Sounds perfect!"

Dan eased out of his chair and said, "When you finish up here I'll have two cots waiting for you in the shelter. You can start at my place 8 a.m. sharp."

Jack nodded, obviously relieved. "Thank you so much," he said, "You don't know how much you're helping us."

Dan just nodded, still smiling. And Hunter had the weirdest suspicion that he was on to them.

That night was the worst of Hunters life, and that was saying something because he'd slept through a lot of bad nights. He kept on thinking he was hearing noises somewhere close by his cot. Once Hunter even thought he saw a shadow move. He promised himself he wouldn't fall asleep. But despite his best efforts he felt his eyelids closing, and before he knew it Hunter was out.

# Hunter

## NY City

Hunter jerked out of bed. Jack was already up and was packing some of their stuff away.

"Get out of bed, now," Jack said urgently, "It's almost eight o'clock."

Hunter rolled out of his cot. The air coming from outside was bitter cold. He helped Jack finish packing up and together they walked over to Dan's house.

Dan was waiting for them to arrive.

"Pleasure to see you again boys," he said.

"It's good to see you too," Jack exclaimed, "Where do we start?"

"Follow me," Dan said, winking at Hunter.

Dan's house was a nice little cottage surrounded by glistening snow. Hunter had to admit that this place was pretty beautiful. Icicles hung from the roof of the cottage, and Hunter could make out a frozen pond in Dan's back yard. Dan escorted them inside and offered them hot chocolate.

"This is the room that needs a little work," he said, "I need to have this drafty old place winterized before I leave."

Hunter found himself stepping into a miniature library. There were three book shelves that lined the walls and four comfy chairs that sat next to a large window that over-looked the yard. The room smelled like peppermint and old books.

Hunter had once had a library in his house back in Chicago. Being in one now made him feel sad and lonely all over again.

Dan smiled warmly as if he could sense Hunter's discomfort.

"So how do you like it?" he asked, "I came to Nova Scotia seeking wilderness and adventure. Now my adventures are mostly here," he gestured vaguely to the book shelves. "I've been around the world and back again and I never had to leave this room."

"You must read a lot," Jack said enthusiastically.

Hunter was pretty sure he had once heard someone say that reading books rots your brain. Or was that television?

"Anyway," Dan said, "There is some plastic sheeting in the corner over there and some tape. Just cover the windows as best you can and try not to leave any gaps. When you're done with that I believe I have a part to contribute in this deal as well."

He took one last sweeping glance of the room and then walked out.

Jack beamed. "This is awesome! We get to work in a library."

Hunter wasn't sure about that, but he nodded anyway and they set to work.

Not two minutes later Hunter was wishing he'd never agreed to this. Jack was a complete book hound, end of story. He ran around the room like he was in love, grabbing books and yelling out random facts. Hunter was the only one who actually did any work.

"Well, I guess there's a first time for everything," Hunter thought as he grabbed a sheet of plastic.

Jack sat at a table reading a book that had the title:

*Critical thinking*

*By Samantha Bright*

"This is really interesting!" Jack exclaimed, "You should read this."

"Sure," Hunter said not paying attention. "Critical thinking, real interesting."

The day went on very slowly after that. Dan had them do other jobs around his house as well, like cleaning out the refrigerator and taking the food to the homeless shelter, and washing his car.

When night finally came Hunter was exhausted. Dan thanked them and walked them back to the shelter. He told them he was leaving tomorrow morning at 7 a.m. sharp.

Hunter lay in his cot and drifted off to sleep. He dreamt he was nine, back in Chicago and his sister was there with him. They were playing in their back yard. The sun was setting and Hunter's mom was calling them in. All of a sudden the dream shifted.

Hunter was in France. He could tell because he was in the basement of their house. There was his sister sitting in the corner. She sat there mumbling things to herself. When she saw him she whispered in a small voice, "Where are you? You ran away." Hunter tried to call out to her but his voice wouldn't work. Then just like that the dream abruptly ended.

Hunter woke with a start. He sat up so hard he almost fell out of the cot. Daylight streamed through the window of the church. Jack lay asleep in the cot next to him.

"Just a dream," Hunter thought, "just a dream."

Once Jack was awake they both got breakfast and sat down at a table.

"There's something I need to talk to you about," Jack whispered, "There was something else in the box I found in my attic."

"What?" Hunter asked, "Another book?"

Jack rolled his eyes. He held up a small envelope and unfolded it to reveal a key with the number 73 etched into the bronze metal.

"A key," Hunter said, "What's it to?"

"That's the million dollar question," he said. "The envelope reads: 92 Delancey Street, New York, NY. It's an address."

"Weird," Hunter said studying the key.

"Weird," Jack replied.

The boys grabbed their bags and walked to Dan's house. Dan didn't notice them at first; he was too busy packing stuff into his car.

"Dan," Jack said.

Dan turned around, smiling. "Morning boys," he said, "Ready to hit the road?"

"Sure," Hunter said, apprehensively. He felt torn. He wanted to get on the road and get out of here. But on the other hand, they barely knew Dan.

Jack hopped into the back seat and Hunter followed.

For the first few minutes Hunter sat on the edge of the seat. He waited for Dan to pull over and mug them. But instead he just talked on and on about Nova Scotia and his adventures there when he was younger. After about thirty minutes, Hunter began to relax.

They drove for hours, stopping for few breaks along the way, and finally arrived at their destination close to midnight. Dan had taken them as far as Newark, NJ and dropped them at the train station where they caught a train into Penn Station. Finally, after what seemed like years, Hunter stepped out onto the pavement of Manhattan.

# Jenifer

## Dumpsters

Jenifer liked living in Manhattan. No one could tell her what to do or where to go. She got lonely sometimes, yes, but everyone gets lonely now and then, right?

Jenifer walked down Pitt Street and turned left onto Rivington. It was late. She had to act natural. Sadly, this tended to be hard for her considering what she wore and where she lived. Of course no one knew where Jenifer lived. If they did… well, that would be really bad. Jenifer's dark black hair came down to her shoulders and her brown eyes shone with confidence.

Finally, she slipped into the alley. It was small, cramped, and full of garbage so most people avoided it. Her mom had obviously thought differently, because Jenifer had grown up here.

Her mom had always told her to be strong and never give up; things would get better. That was all Jenifer had ever known - that things would somehow, against all odds, get better. Even after her mom died and left her alone, she never stopped believing.

Yes, people did call her crazy and laugh at her sometimes because she was homeless. But, from Jenifer's perspective, things would someday get better.

Jenifer walked along the cracked pavement heading for the end of the alley.

Suddenly she heard something. Voices. Two people were obviously arguing about something. Jenifer slipped behind a dumpster and listened intently.

"We have to figure out a plan," a male voice was saying.

Jenifer could see shadows moving along the wall. "What if they found her hide out?" she thought, "And why were they in this alley?" More movement, and then the second voice spoke.

"But Jack, we found the street. All we have to do is go into that bank."

"Bank?" Jenifer thought. That sounded like a big uh-oh.

The guy who's name was Jack grumbled, but agreed to go to the bank. Jenifer could hear their footsteps getting closer to the dumpster. A few more seconds and they'd be right on top of her. She had to act, and act fast.

She had dealt with plenty of people like this before. People with absolutely no street smarts whatsoever. She decided to have a little fun. She stepped out into the open alley, revealing herself. She could now see that there were two boys who looked to be about the same age as her.

Both boys jumped back in surprise. The shorter boy gasped, "What the…"

"Oh, hello. Are you looking for something?" Jenifer said cheerfully.

"Umm…who are you?" the other boy asked. Jenifer immediately noticed that he had striking blue eyes. So much so, that she had to look away. Finally, she regained her confidence.

"I'm Jenifer. I overheard that you're looking for the bank, right?"

"What else did you hear? Do you just spend your nights hiding behind dumpsters listening to other peoples conversations?" the shorter boy asked, angrily.

"Oh, no. I live here," Jenifer replied.

"Wait, what? You *live* here? Behind the dumpster?" asked the boy with the blue eyes.

"No, no." Jenifer answered, rolling her eyes. "I live up there," she went on, gesturing to an old darkened brick building.

"How can you live there? It looks abandoned," said the boy.

"It is. Anyway, why do you want to get into the bank? You're not seriously thinking of breaking in, are you?" Jenifer asked.

Both boys glanced at each other nervously.

"We were just planning on going in and... you know..."

Jenifer raised her eye brows.

"No I don't know. What were you planning on doing?"

"Well..."

"You know," Jenifer said smiling, "I could help you get in."

"We are not here to steal anything," the boy with the blue eyes said flatly, "If you don't mind I think we'll be on our way."

He grabbed the shorter boys arm and they started to walk away.

"I bet your hungry," Jenifer said. "I have some food."

"Really?" the shorter boy asked, suddenly interested.

"Yes, and it's not from the dumpster either," she said, laughing. "But I'm not willing to share anything with you unless you tell me your names first."

"I'm Hunter and this is my friend Jack," the shorter boy offered. Jenifer sensed right away from their brief interaction that Hunter was more impulsive than his friend Jack. Jack seemed deep in thought, and cautious about talking.

Jenifer led the way through the alley, up a fire escape ladder, and into the dark brick building. Once inside, she lit a small lantern. This had been home for the past several months. All she owned were the items in her backpack, the lantern, and several blankets she had laid over thick cardboard to make a comfortable bed. She watched carefully as Jack and Hunter looked around, uneasily.

She pulled several apples, some cheese, salami and bread out of her backpack. "Compliments of the corner deli," she said. "Help yourself."

Hunter grinned. "Thanks," he said.

Jack didn't take anything to eat. Instead he looked around the old brick room suspiciously. "So," he exclaimed nervously, "how long have you lived here?"

"Oh, I don't know… a few months," Jenifer said shrugging. "Ever since my mom died a few years ago I've been moving around a lot. But I like it here. Where do you live?"

Jack looked at her quizzically. "England," he replied.

Jenifer nodded, although she felt a little suspicious herself. What was a kid from England doing in an alley in Manhattan? "Ok," she said changing the subject, "You need to get to the bank because…?"

"Long story," Hunter said through a bite of bread.

"Yeah," Jack said, "Trust me. You don't want to get involved."

Jenifer raised her eye brows. "Hey, my weekend was going to be boring. If you need help with anything…" she trailed off.

Jack and Hunter exchanged looks.

"Admit it Jack," Hunter sighed, "We have no idea what we're doing. We barely made it to Manhattan. I think she can help us."

Jack must have realized he was out numbered because he said, "You can help us get into the bank and that's it."

"Great," Jenifer said, "Tell me what I need to know."

# Jenifer

## The Roach

Jack didn't really seem like he wanted to tell Jenifer everything. From what she could understand he was adopted and had run away from home. Jack had found an envelope with a key in it, and the envelope had an address on it.

"And so you're telling me," Jenifer asked, "That the address on the envelope is the same one as the bank across the street?"

Jack nodded. "And we think that the key goes to a safety deposit box inside the bank."

"It makes sense," Hunter put in.

"Ok, let me get this straight," Jenifer said, "You want me to tell you how to open a safety deposit box with that key?"

"Yes," Jack said, "All we're asking for is advise."

Jenifer shook her head. "It's not possible."

"Wait. What?" Hunter said, "It's got to be possible."

"Illegally, yes," Jenifer explained. "But if you just plan on waltzing in there and trying to open a safety deposit box, good luck."

"Well then, how do we do it Miss Know-It-All?" Jack said angrily.

"Simple," Jenifer said, "Considering the fact that your parents are dead and you have no other living relative, then you inherit the box. But you can't open it until you're eighteen years old. So an easy solution would be to wait a couple of years."

"Or?" Jack asked.

"Or, if you have a legal guardian, they can come in with you and open the box. The guardian would have to show ID and you would have to show your birth certificate," Jenifer said.

Jack shook his head in despair. "It's hopeless," he moaned.

"Not exactly," Jenifer said, I've got a friend who lives around here. He's easy to find, and I've got a feeling he'll be up for this job. He can make a very convincing ID."

"Hold on a sec," Hunter said standing up, "You think we should fake an ID so we can get into the bank? Isn't that illegal?"

"That's sort of the point," Jenifer said. She was starting to get annoyed by these boys. They obviously had never lived on the streets before.

Jack stood up also. He looked kind of weird with his black hair and electric blue eyes. As if someone had taken a bunch of miss-matched human features and morphed them together.

"I need to get into that box," he said plainly. "If this is the only way to get in... then I'm taking it."

Hunter looked back and forth between Jack and Jenifer as if he was trying to decide who was more insane. "But who's ID are we going to fake?"

"My only legal guardian," Jack said, "My parents back in England."

"Exactly," Jenifer said nodding.

"Great," Hunter said, "Now I'm going to become a wanted criminal."

"Well, then," Jenifer exclaimed, "We've got work to do."

They had been talking most of the night and agreed to lay down and try to get a few hours of sleep. By the time they awoke, it was nearly noon.

Finding Roach was easy; he liked to hang out around the soup kitchen. Jenifer led the way around the corner of the building where they found a short stubby little man. He was just sitting there in plain sight holding a bowl of soup and a piece of bread. His tattered clothes made it obvious he was homeless.

"Roach!" Jenifer called.

The man looked up from his bowl of soup and gave her a toothless grin.

"Jenifer," he said standing, "Just the person I wanted to see. I'll be needin' my payment from the work I did for you."

"Roach, I already paid you. Besides, that's not why I'm here. I need you to help me with something."

He frowned. "I'm not helping you until you give me that buck you owe me," he said slumping back down into his chair.

Then Jack stepped forward and looked Roach right in the face. "We need help," he said, "And I'd be happy to pay you much more than a buck for your cooperation." Jack pulled out a twenty dollar bill from his bag. Much more than Jenifer had seen in a long time.

Well that got Roach's attention. He sat forward and smiled slyly like he had just told a funny joke. "What's the job kid?"

Jack explained to Roach what he wanted him to do for them.

When he was done Roach just nodded like the problem amused him. "All right, all right, I'll do it," he said, "But first give me the dough."

Jenifer had learned not to trust Roach when it came to money. "After," she said, "First get us into the bank and back out safely. Then and only then will we give you your money."

"Fine," Roach sighed, "Then give me the information instead. Although the money would be better," he mumbled.

Jack rattled off his parent's information while Roach wrote it down on a grimey note pad. Hunter kept on twiddling his thumbs and looking eagerly at the diner across the road. Jenifer couldn't help but wonder how these two boys who were so different had become friends.

"Right," Roach said, "I'll have the ID ready by tomorrow afternoon. Be right here at this spot around lunch time. Oh, and make sure you bring the dough," he said smiling, "I like my money fresh."

"Of course," Jack said rolling his eyes, "I'll keep that in mind."

"Excellent," Roach said smiling wider and not even noticing the slightest bit of sarcasm in Jack's voice.

"Yo, Jack," Hunter said, "You don't think we could... you know..." He pointed to the diner across the road. "I could really use a bacon cheese burger."

"You just ate!" Jack said.

"Come on you guys," Jenifer said smiling, "We should get back, and plan."

Jack looked pretty happy for an excuse to get away from Roach.

As they walked away from the soup kitchen Roach called from behind them, "Don't forget the money."

# Jenifer

## Forward

On the walk back to Jenifer's place Jack seemed a lot friendlier. He didn't seem as scared of Jenifer as he had earlier. Finally, she got up the courage to ask a question that had been bothering her.

"How did you get that twenty dollar bill?" Jenifer asked.

Jack looked down as if he wasn't sure what to say. "That's none of your business," he said, "Come on. We've got to plan."

"Oh, right…" Jenifer trailed off.

Jack had already walked ahead. Hunter and Jenifer walked along through the crowds of people that swarmed the streets of Manhattan.

"You've got to give him a break," Hunter said, "He just found out he was adopted a week ago. I think he's still getting over the shock of things."

Jenifer just nodded. But she felt hollow inside.

"He knows what's in the box doesn't he?" Jenifer whispered.

"I… I think Jack thinks it's a message from his parents," Hunter replied. Hunter put a hand on her shoulder. "He'll be fine," he said, "Besides we've got bigger problems to worry about."

Jenifer took a deep breath. She knew Hunter was trying to make her feel better but all she felt was dread. She had been in the same position Jack was in a few years ago. Jenifer had been waiting for a sign; something that her mom had left. A message, something, anything that she could fall back on. But finally the day came when she realized that a message wasn't coming. Her mom was dead, and she had to move on.

"Right," Jenifer said, forcing a confident smile, "Bigger problems..."

Jack, Hunter and Jenifer emerged on Patchogue Road. The sun was sinking in the sky and Jenifer could tell that Jack and Hunter were as tired as she was.

They climbed up the fire escape ladder and into the dark brick room where Jenifer lit a small lantern. Jack's mood hadn't changed since their walk back. He seemed suspicious of Jenifer again like she might turn into some sort of fire breathing dragon.

Hunter was trying to be enthusiastic about everything. He told corny jokes and tried to lighten everyone's mood but Jenifer could see his heart wasn't in it.

The night dragged on until it was at least midnight. They had stayed up all night planning and acting out their parts. If this was going to work, Jenifer thought, it was going to have to be very convincing.

By the time Jenifer had given Jack and Hunter their own cardboard sleeping pad she was so tired she had to force herself not to collapse on the spot. Hunter fell asleep as soon as his head hit his "pillow" but Jack just laid there, his eyes wide open.

"You… you ok," Jenifer asked hesitantly.

"Yes," Jack answered still looking at the ceiling, "I'm fine."

Hunter mumbled something in his sleep about a bacon cheese burger.

"I'm sorry about your parents," she said, "they obviously mean a lot to you." Jenifer was afraid she had really done it. What was she thinking? He'd already shown that he didn't want to talk about it.

Instead Jack just sighed. "I think Hunter was right," he said, "We have no idea what we're doing any more. I'm not sure if I'm doing the right thing, breaking into that box."

"I know how you feel," Jenifer said, "But with stuff like this there's only one way to go."

Jack nodded. "Forward."

"Forward," Jenifer agreed.

And to her surprise Jack smiled. "You get us through this, dumpster girl, and maybe you're not as bad as I thought."

Jenifer beamed. She put her head on her "pillow" and instantly fell asleep.

# Jenifer

## Clothes Donation

Jenifer memorized the plan. It wasn't very hard and she didn't have a very big part to play. Jack was the one with the hard part. He had to go in and pretend to be Roach's son (that would give anyone the jitters), while Roach pretended to be Jack's British dad. Hunter and Jenifer would wait outside and keep guard. Jenifer didn't really see any reason that anyone would have to keep guard, but she trusted Jack's judgment.

"Remember, stick to the plan," Jack said as they walked back toward the soup kitchen.

Although Jenifer got the feeling he was talking more to himself than anyone else.

"I've got one question," Hunter asked, "what happens if the plan doesn't work?"

"Don't worry. The plan *is* going to work because no one's going to mess up, right?" Jenifer said.

"Oh… right," Hunter said nodding.

"Um… guys," Jack said, "I think I found the Roach."

Jenifer looked up and saw that Jack was right. Roach was running toward them pushing past crowds of people. His ratty clothes and crazy smile made him look like a cross between a roadside hippy and an insane walrus.

"Yep," Hunter exclaimed, "that's definitely our Roach."

Roach caught up to them and gave Jenifer a smile. Then he turned to Jack. "Well," Roach said frowning at him, "You're late."

"Did you do it?" Jack asked, ignoring Roach.

"Not here!" Roach hissed, "Too many people."

"How about we go to the diner?" Hunter put in helpfully.

"No," Jenifer said, "way too many people."

"The soup kitchen," Jack said. He looked at Roach. "Why didn't you wait for us?"

"Sorry," Roach said, "Just… you know… that twenty dollar bill... I guess I got a little excited."

"Dude!" Hunter said, "Will you forget the twenty dollar bill!"

"Come on guys," Jack said, "I am not going to get arrested. We are going to do this and do it right."

"Jack's right," Jenifer said, "Let's get to the soup kitchen and explain the plan to Roach."

When they arrived at the soup kitchen it wasn't very crowded, so Jenifer, Jack, Hunter, and Roach all sat down at a table comfortably.

"What's the plan?" Roach asked.

Jack glanced behind him to make sure no one was listening. "Ok," he said, "Step one, we all get a change of clothes."

"All right!" Roach said, "I'm liking the sound of this plan!"

Again Jack ignored him. "Step two, me and Roach go into the bank, open the box and walk out without getting arrested."

"Is that it?" Roach said.

"Well, Hunter and Jenifer will wait outside just in case… umm…" Jack glanced behind him again. "Just in case anyone shows up," he finished.

Hunter shot Jack a look that said something like… "Not now."

"So," Jenifer said breaking the silence, "Roach, you did your part?"

He nodded and held up an ID card for them to see.

"Excellent," Jack said, "And I've got my birth certificate. All we have to do now is get some new clothes and open that box."

Jenifer knew where to get clothes. Her mother had shown her how to do it many times. The trick was to wait until no one was looking and then quickly grab whatever you needed.

"You're joking right?" Jack asked as they walked up to the metal box behind the diner.

On the side of the box were big black letters:

*Clothes Donation*

Even Hunter seemed a little uneasy about the idea.

"All right," Jenifer said, "Roach..."

Roach looked behind him and then plunged his hand into the slot in the top of the box.

He came up with a little girl's shirt that said... *Life is sweet!*

"Ummm, I don't think so," Hunter said trying not to laugh.

Finally after a few minutes of rummaging around through the box, Roach found what he was looking for.

"Well," Jack said looking Roach over, "I guess it's the best we can do."

Roach wore a tweed suit jacket, dress pants and only slightly torn dress shoes.

"It's definitely an improvement," Jenifer said.

"Only one last thing," Jack said. He threw Roach a brown leather wallet. "You can put the ID in there."

Roach opened the wallet eagerly. "Darn it! Where's the money?" he asked.

"You can have the money," Jenifer said trying to keep her voice calm, "When you get us in and out of the bank." Roach was really starting to annoy her.

"Fine," Roach said, "Let's get this over with."

"Bank time?" Hunter asked, looking wearily at the large brick building across the road.

"Bank time," Jack agreed.

Five minutes later Jack, Hunter, Jenifer and Roach were staring up at the letters above the building:

*Bank of America*

"Well, this is it," Jenifer said. She had never heard her voice come out so weak. She had to pull it together! What was it that her mom used to say? "Be strong and never give up."

"Well this is it," Jenifer said a little louder.

"Well," Jack said, "Here goes nothing."

Jack nodded to Jenifer, gave Hunter a high five and then stepped into the bank.

# Jenifer

## Bright

Jenifer and Hunter stood outside watching the door eagerly. How long ago was it that Jack had gone in? Five minutes maybe? Or ten? It was hard to tell. What if Jack was caught? All of these questions were swimming around in Jenifer's head.

"Is that your mom's?"

Jenifer looked up. She had almost forgotten that Hunter was still standing there.

"What?" Jenifer asked.

"That," Hunter replied, pointing at Jenifer.

At first she didn't understand, but then Jenifer looked down and realized that she had been fiddling with her locket.

"Your mom was a philosopher, right?" Hunter asked, "Samantha Bright."

Jenifer was stunned. No one had ever, *ever* figured this much out about her mom. Let alone her. She was nobody. Just a homeless kid who lived on the streets.

"How…" she began. Jenifer's mouth felt like sandpaper.

"Me and Jack were at a library," Hunter explained. "Jack was reading this book about critical thinking. The authors name was Samantha Bright."

"But... how..." Jenifer said again.

"Your locket says Samantha Bight," Hunter pressed, "I'm guessing when your mom died she left it to you."

"Umm..." Jenifer finally unstuck her mouth. "Yeah," she said, "Yeah, that's exactly what happened." Jenifer made a mental note not to underestimate Hunter again. He was obviously a lot smarter than he looked. She wondered if Hunter had figured anything else out about her. "We used to live in an apartment around here," Jenifer said, "My mom wrote a couple of books but we didn't have enough money to keep living there. And then she got sick..." Jenifer said, trailing off.

"So you started living out on the streets," Hunter said, "And then your mom died and..."

"Yeah," Jenifer said, weakly.

"Sorry," Hunter said nervously, "I shouldn't have brought up the topic."

"No... no it's ok, it's just..." Jenifer didn't know what to say. She had never opened herself up like this before.

"I'm really sorry," Hunter said, "I didn't want to upset you."

"It's fine," Jenifer said forcing a confident smile.

"Here," Hunter said sticking out his hand, "We haven't properly met. I'm Hunter Truman."

"Jenifer Bright," Jenifer said.

They shook hands a little awkwardly. They both stood there studying each other for a long time until Jenifer finally spoke. "I'm worried about Jack," she said, "What if they get arrested?"

"Aw, he'll be fine," Hunter replied, "I'm worried about Roach. If anyone is going to mess this up, it's going to be him."

Jenifer nodded thoughtfully.

"Can I ask you something?" Hunter said, "Why are you doing this for us?"

Jenifer looked up at him. "Because I'm your friend, Burger Boy, so get used to it."

# Jack

## The Bank

Jack had to say he'd never been in a bank before. For one thing it was big and very, very bright. Sunlight poured through windows on either side of him so he had to hold his hand over his eyes. Roach walked alongside Jack messing with his jacket.

"Leave it alone," Jack hissed.

The bank teller looked up at them.

"Why, hello sir!" He said cheerfully, "How may I help you?"

"We're here to open this kid's something or other box," Roach replied.

The man raised an eyebrow.

"I would like to access my safety deposit box," Jack said, ignoring Roach's comment.

"Identification," the teller said. His good mood had vanished.

Roach took out the ID he had made and placed it on the table. The teller examined it and then punched a few buttons on his computer.

"No…" he said, "No, there is no safety deposit box under this name."

"It's mine," Jack said cautiously, "This is my legal guardian."

"Yours?" exclaimed the teller, "But you're only a child."

"My parents died," Jack explained calmly, "We only found out about the box recently. I have a birth certificate to prove it."

Jack held out the slip of yellowed paper he had found in his attic for the teller to see.

The teller examined it and then his face went white. "Ju… just a minute," he stammered, "I must have a word with my manager." He scuttled out of the room hastily.

When he had left, Roach grinned at Jack. "We're doing great!" he said enthusiastically.

"We!" Jack said angrily, "I'm doing everything!"

"Keep your pants on," Roach said cracking his knuckles, "This isn't over yet!"

Jack rolled his eyes. "Sure thing Pops."

About five minutes later the teller walked back up to the desk followed by another man. The new man was stout with straight brown hair and a jacket like Roach's, although his looked a lot nicer. Jack guessed he must be the manager.

"May I please see your ID again, sir?" the manager asked extending his hand.

"Course you can!" Roach said. "Oh, and by the way, I like your taste in clothing."

The manager examined Roach's ID and then punched more buttons into his computer.

"George Miller is it?" He asked looking at the screen.

Jack nudged Roach. "Oh… yeah! My name is George." Roach said.

"Please sir," the teller said nervously, "This child is very young. Maybe another time-"

"Nonsense," said the manager, "We have a box under his parent's name, and he's here with his legal guardian. I see no reason to not allow him to access his box."

The teller looked really nervous now. Jack wondered why he didn't want them to get in to the box.

Jack also felt bad about leaving Hunter and Jenifer outside by themselves. After he had met Jenifer, Jack had had a long conversation with Hunter in French. Hunter had told Jack that he had been seeing shadows at night, ever since Nova Scotia. Jack had said that it was probably just his imagination but last night Jack could have sworn he'd seen a shadow outside the window. Jack hadn't talked about it with Hunter but he knew he had come to the same conclusion.

"Take them back, Robert," the manager said nodding to the teller. And with that, he left the room.

"Do you have your key?" the teller asked, glaring at Jack.

Jack held up the small bronze key with the number *73* on it.

"Fine," the teller grumbled, "This way if you please, Mr. Callow."

The teller led the way to the back of the bank and into a small room. He opened the door, let them in and then closed the door behind him. The room was filled with hundreds of small boxes, or drawers, that seemed to be part of the wall itself.

"73... 73..." The teller said, "Ah, here..." He walked over to a box at the end of the sixth row. "Key," he said, "Come on! We don't have all day!"

As Jack handed the teller the key he couldn't help but notice how uneasy the guy was acting. But on the other hand, Jack felt uneasy himself. What if there was nothing in the box? He hoped it would be a message from his parents. But did he really want to know?

The teller placed the key in the hole. Jack held his breath... it fit! Next the teller pulled out another key.

"What's that?" Jack asked curiously.

"You keep one key. The bank keeps the other," the teller explained impatiently. "That way, the only individual who can open the box is the owner, with the official approval of the bank."

"Interesting," Roach said, obviously not interested, "Now get on with it, I want that dough."

Jack kicked him in the shin.

"OW! What was that for?"

"Will you shut up!" Jack roared.

The teller was watching this exchange. He raised an eyebrow.

"Anyway," Jack said carefully, "We were in a hurry?"

"Yes, of course," the teller said turning back to the box. He fit in the last key and then took them both out.

"I have to leave now," the teller said reluctantly, "I'm not allowed to be in here when you open the box."

"Oh, sure," Jack said happy to get rid of this guy. He was starting to creep him out.

The teller walked out of the room and was about to go when he turned back. "Beware Jack Callow," he said, "If you open that box you will most certainly have a dangerous future ahead of you. Sometimes it is best to be ignorant."

And with that, he shut the door leaving Jack and Roach inside a room full of small metal boxes.

Jack stood there, shocked. This whole thing was getting more bizarre by the minute. Jack didn't know what the teller's message meant but one thing as for sure. The man obviously thought that there was something bad in that box. Did Jack really want to know what it was? It would be a shame to have come this far and not even try.

"Here goes nothing," Jack said, and he slid open the lid…

# Jack

## SPQR

The lid opened easily and inside lay a piece of old paper. Nothing more, nothing less. Jack picked it up gingerly as if it were about to explode. He turned it over and instantaneously knew what it was.

"The… the book," Jack said, his hand trembling. It was a page from the book. Why was it in the safety deposit box? Jack tucked it safely inside his coat pocket. He had to be careful with Roach around. But Jack promised himself that he would look at it later, when he had time to examine it.

"Wow…" Roach said staring at Jack. "That's what you came all this way to get? A piece of paper?"

"Um… yeah, I guess," Jack said. He wasn't sure what to say. What did this book mean and why was he involved? He walked up to the front desk and retrieved his key from the teller.

The man didn't say anything but the look in his eye told Jack that he was beyond angry. He was furious. The teller had not wanted Jack to get into that box and Jack had a feeling he had a good reason. The walk back outside was a daze. It seemed to take forever for Jack to move one foot in front of the other.

Hunter and Jenifer were waiting for him outside.

"So?" Jenifer said eagerly, "Did you get inside the box? What was in there?"

"Later," Jack whispered. "Not here. Too many people."

"Right," Hunter said glancing behind his shoulder, "Too many people."

"Ahem," Roach said, "The money?"

Jack reluctantly took out the twenty dollar bill that Dan had given him before he'd dropped them off at Penn Station.

"Here's the dough," Jack said sarcastically, handing Roach the bill.

"All right!" Roach exclaimed, "I'm going to buy some more suits!"

Hunter rolled his eyes. "Have fun with that," he said.

Roach ran off happily down the street, swinging his arms at his side.

"Good riddance," Hunter mumbled.

Jenifer elbowed him. "He got us into the bank Hunter. He's not all bad."

"Now you're sticking up for him?" Hunter asked, "How can you? He's such a... a-"

"A roach?" Jack suggested.

"Yes, a roach," Hunter agreed.

Jenifer laughed out loud. "Roach the roach," she said shaking her head. "Makes perfect sense."

"Come on," Jack said, "There's something I need to show you. Besides I think dumpster girl deserves an explanation."

A few minutes later Jack stood staring up at the old brick building that lingered like a storm cloud above him. To him it looked haunted and he could never seem to wrap his mind around the fact that Jenifer lived here. This was her home.

As Jack made his way up the fire escape ladder he thought he saw a figure move behind the dumpster. Was he just imagining things? Jack climbed faster up the ladder just to be sure. Hunter and Jenifer were already inside waiting for him.

"So what is it that you wanted to show us," Jenifer asked.

"First things first," Jack said as he sat down on his cardboard bed, "I need to explain things."

And he did, starting with his day at school and ending when he met Jenifer. Hunter interjected a few times to correct Jack. But he got the feeling that Hunter was trying to make himself sound a lot more heroic than he really was.

"And then I stepped in with a quick jab to the left and that security guard became shish kabob!" Hunter said imitating the movement.

Jenifer didn't say anything at all, she just listened intently.

"And so we made it to Manhattan and found the bank," Jack finished.

"And you have no idea what this book is and for some reason this Ross guy wants it?" Jenifer asked.

Exactly, Jack said. He took the book out from his bag and opened it.

"Nothing," Hunter said, "It's blank."

"Blank?" Jenifer asked, "Then why does Ross want it?"

"I don't know," Jack said, "But look at this." Jack ran his finger along the binding. There were marks on the side of the blank page next to the binding as if someone had ripped a page out.

Jenifer sat up straight.

"I'm going to take a wild guess here," she said, "But I've got a feeling you found a page to this book in the box."

Jack nodded and took out the page he had found in the safety deposit box. It felt rough in his hand. Jack hadn't even looked at it yet but he could tell there was writing on it. "Please," he thought, "Be a message from my parents, I want to know." Jack flipped the page over and Hunter and Jenifer leaned closer.

The words on the page were written in fancy script.

*Enter the chamber where even for the hero the only exit is death. SPQR*

*Washington*

Jack and Jenifer looked at each other.

"Uh...," Hunter said, "What chamber? And does that mean, *George* Washington?"

Jack stood up and started pacing the room. This was obviously a riddle and Jack knew the answer. But could it really be that easy? Was this a message from his parents? If so why didn't they just write it out in plain English? Jack wondered if this was a test.

"I don't know about the signature," Jack said. His heart was thumping fast. "But I know the answer to this riddle. The big clue is SPQR."

"What does it mean?" Jenifer asked standing up as well.

"Senatus Populusque Romanus," Jack said triumphantly.

"Guzundite!" Hunter said.

Jenifer stared at him. "Was that Latin?" She asked obviously impressed.

"Yes," Jack said, "It means The Senate of Rome."

"Ok," Hunter said nodding unsurely, "What the heck does that have to do with anything?"

"It was the motto for the old Roman Empire," Jack explained.

"Cool!" Hunter said sarcastically, "Now can you tell me what the top part says?"

Jack met Jenifer's eyes and he knew she'd figured it out as well.

"Enter the place were even for the hero the only exit is death," Jenifer whispered.

Jack nodded.

"Gladiators!" They both said together.

"Glada what?" Hunter asked.

"Here," Jenifer said.

She slipped off her back pack and removed the contents. There wasn't much, just a flashlight some apples and a few books. Jenifer picked up one of the books and opened it. She began to read.

***<u>The Colosseum</u>***

*"The Colosseum's Construction (originally called the Amphitheatrum Flavium) was ordered by Emperor Vespasian circa 70 A.D., and it was completed in 80 A.D., during Titus' reign. It was built on the site of the Golden House–"*

"Will you get to the point?" Hunter said irritably, "Skip ahead!"

"Well *sorry,*" Jenifer said raising her eyebrows at Jack, as if to say "What's his problem?"

*"The Colosseum was also a venue for gladiatorial contests,"* Jenifer continued. "*Gladiators were normally slaves, foreign captives, or criminals. But some free citizens did volunteer for gladiatorial duty.*

*Over the centuries different styles of gladiators developed, each with its own unique outfit and weaponry. Gladiators were carefully matched against one another to make sure there was even contest between fighters. A gladiator went into the arena expecting to kill or be killed.*

The room was silent.

"I need to get to the Colosseum," Jack said walking to the window.

"Whoa, whoa, whoa!" Hunter said, "What if it's a trap or something? What if Ross-"

"I need to get to the Colosseum," Jack repeated, "It may be the only way I can find out more."

"Hold on a sec bro," Hunter said, "You find this book and then you find out your parents are dead and then you find another page from the book telling you to go to the Colosseum. Don't you think that's a little suspicious?"

"Umm," Jack said. He didn't know what to say. His mind felt like an over inflated balloon. Jack had to get to Rome. The only problem was he didn't have any money. And it was then that Jack realized he was starving. He hadn't eaten all day!

"Look at this!" Jenifer yelled excitedly.

Jack looked up and found that Jenifer had been examining the paper.

"Look at this signature," She said holding out the paper for Jack and Hunter to see. "It has a mark after Washington."

Jack squinted at the paper and saw that Jenifer was right. There was a mark after Washington. It looked like a triangle with an eye inside of it.

"I've seen that before!" Hunter said, "But I can't remember where."

"So have I!" Jenifer blurted.

"No…" Jack said, still staring at the mark, "I've never seen anything like it before."

"Ahh," Hunter said putting his hand to his temple, "Where have I seen that mark?"

"Here," Jack said taking the page from Jenifer. He tucked it into the book and stuffed the book in his bag. "I'm going to find a way to get to the Colosseum," Jack said, "You guys stay here and–"

"We're coming with you," Jenifer said abruptly.

"Yes, of course," Hunter said stepping forward.

Jack didn't want them to come. What if it was a trap? Then it would be his fault. Although they had come this far together - even Jenifer. Jack didn't want to admit it, but he needed their help.

"Fine," Jack decided, "You can come with me. But if it's a trap and umm… we, you know, get trapped, don't blame me."

"Great," Jenifer said smiling, "We need to get to Rome."

# Jack

## The Return of Mr. Evil Glowing Eyes

Ok, let's just say that getting to Rome didn't work out so well.

"I think we misjudged the distance a little," Hunter panted as they walked helplessly back across the Williamsburg Bridge. They had been trying to make their way to LaGuardia airport, hoping to somehow catch a ride, but to no avail.

None of them knew exactly what they were going to do once they got to the airport. They had absolutely no money at all. But they had decided to first just get to an airport and then come up with a plan.

The winter air cut at Jacks frozen hands like a knife. "This is hopeless," Jack said shivering. "Let's just turn back and rethink this whole thing."

"I know a place we can get warm and talk. Under the bridge," Jenifer said.

"Please, just no more dumpsters," Hunter pleaded as they followed her under the bridge.

When they got out of the cold Jenifer rounded on Jack. "This is crazy! What if the answer's not even in Rome?" she said.

Hunter flinched at the word crazy. Jack had almost forgotten about Hunter's sister. Remembering it made him feel even worse.

"We'll find a way," Jack said, "We just need more time-"

"We've got all the time in the world Jack! We've got time to kill. What we need is money!" Jenifer said, "Jack, think about it. Rome? What do you expect to find there?"

Jack knew that she was right. Earlier, going to Rome sounded like such a good idea. There was that small amount of hope that maybe his parents were trying to tell him something.

"I'm sorry," Jenifer said putting a hand on his shoulder, "We'll find a way."

Jack could tell she was trying to make him feel better, but all he felt was dread. He had come all this way. He was not going to back down so easily.

"Look out!" Hunter suddenly yelled.

Jack whirled around and saw the worst site ever. Roach was speeding toward them, yelling like a lunatic. His new suit was flapping in the wind.

"Get out of the way!" he yelled, pushing Hunter down.

Roach sped past Jack and Jenifer and dove behind a metal trash can.

"What the-"

Hunter never finished his sentence because standing in front him was a man. A man with a scarred face and gnarled hands that were holding a gun. But the worse part of all were his bright, intelligent green eyes.

"Hello Jack," Ross said, "Long time, no see."

Jack was stunned. All those shadows...

"DOWN!" Jack yelled and he tackled Jenifer to the ground just as Ross fired his gun.

Hunter dove violently to the left and slammed into Roach who was cowering behind the trash can.

"HA! HA! HA!" Ross yelled in his psycho voice. "Come out, come out! I need that book!"

"Is that-" Jenifer asked.

"Yeah," Jack whispered.

More shots were fired and Jack and Jenifer hurled themselves out of the line of fire, slamming into Hunter. Roach screamed. "You can have the dough kid, just get me outta here!"

"Great," Jack thought, "We're completely defenseless and about to be destroyed by a mad man."

Ross walked casually toward them swinging his gun in the air. "The answer lies in Rome," he said delighted, "But where in Rome?" He fixed his green eyes on Jack. "You still don't know who you are, do you Jack

Callow? Ignorance is best. Hand over the book and you can go free."

Suddenly the teller's warning came flooding back into Jack's mind. It was somehow connected...

"You know that bank teller, don't you?" Jack said standing up, "He told you where I was, and he told you to follow us, didn't he?"

Ross smiled. "Now your catching on, you little brat."

"This book leads to something," Jack said, "And you're after it. What does it lead to?"

"Good, good," Ross said not even caring to answer Jack's question.

"Tell me!" Jack shouted. "Where does it lead? And if you know who I am then tell me!"

"You'll never know who you are!" Ross shouted back, "Because I'll kill you before you figure it out!" He shot more bullets at Jack but Jack was expecting it this time. He jumped backward and forced himself back against the bridge abutment. If Jack had moved a split second later he would have been dead.

"Tell me!" Jack shouted again.

Ross was about to shoot a third round when he doubled over in pain. "AHHH! You stupid girl!"

Jack realized what had happened. Jenifer had snuck up behind Ross and hit him in the back of the head with her back pack. Ross held his head in pain and

Jack had just enough time to leap back over to Hunter and Roach. Now Ross stood between Jenifer and Jack. Jenifer's dark brown eyes were filled with terror.

"Give me the book or she dies!" Ross screeched, still holding his head. He had his gun aimed at Jenifer's face. "3! 2!-"

"Wait!" Hunter yelled.

"No!" Jack screamed.

"1!"

BANG! BANG! BANG!

Jack didn't know how but Jenifer managed to dodge the first two bullets by twisting in mid-air. The third one… well she wasn't so lucky. The bullet grazed her leg and Jenifer fell down… down… down… Thankfully she was able to put her hands out to break the fall, but still…

Jack's face was white with horror. Ross smirked. "Hand over the book boy, before I finish her."

Jack needed to get to Rome. This book was the only thing he had to go on, but he was not going to let Jenifer die. Jack slipped off his bag and took out the book. "You can have it," he said, "But first everyone here except me and you leaves, and I will give you the book alone."

Ross's smile faded. "Well, what prevents me from just shooting you right now?"

"Because I have more information that I won't tell you unless you do what I say," Jack said.

Jack could see that Jenifer was bleeding now and he knew he had to hurry.

"You're bluffing," Ross decided.

"Shoot me," Jack said calmly, "And find out."

Ross squinted at Jack. "Okay... okay Jack Callow. We'll do this your way, this time,"

The way he said *this time* sent a chill up Jack's spine. Ross set down his gun and took a step backward. Hunter walked over to Jenifer and helped her up. She stumbled and fell again.

"I... I can't," she said trying to lift her head. Scarlet blood soaked her jeans.

It took some time but finally Jenifer was able to stand on one foot although she was still leaning heavily on Hunter's shoulder. They hobbled off followed by Roach who was still cowering.

Jack was angry now. Who did Ross think he was, shooting at his friends like that? Jack wanted to smack him in the face but he could tell Ross was a lot stronger than him. Not to mention that he was a head taller.

Jack was about to hand Ross the book and make a run for it when he heard the sound of pounding footsteps.

"Please no," Jack thought, "No more trouble."

Of course he was wrong. Two figures appeared in the distance.

One was a girl who looked a little older than Jack. The other was a rather large, heavy-set looking guy. The girl had flowing blond hair and a very weary, solemn face. She wore jeans, a leather jacket, and a brightly colored scarf around her neck. The guy on the other hand looked about in his mid-thirties and wore black everything, as if he were trying to blend into the shadows. (Or his mum's pancakes.) He had on shades so Jack couldn't see his eyes. He looked exactly like an undercover detective. They both held guns and Jack found that rather odd considering the fact that the girl looked only about sixteen. Maybe they were cops in training?

"What's going on here?" the girl asked pointing her gun at Ross, "Some people back there said they were being attacked, and one of them is injured."

"Yes," Jack said quickly, recovering from his shock.

So many things had just happened at once. Ross seemed to be examining the situation the way you would in chess.

The girl glanced at Jack and gestured for him to move behind her. Jack did this with no hesitation. He wanted to say something to Ross like, "See ya, sucker!" but Jack decided against it.

"Go!" the girl said to Ross, "Before I shoot!"

Ross clenched his fists and shot Jack a look of pure hatred. "I'm going to kill you kid!" he yelled at Jack, "Just you wait and see!"

"Move!" the girl said.

Ross held his hands up and walked slowly past them, the girl aiming her gun at him the whole time. When he reached the side of the bridge, Ross ran from sight.

# Jack

## The Mark

Jack was too stunned to even register what had just happened. He turned around and realized what a commotion they had started. There was a loose ring of homeless people who had stopped to watch the action. Jack also heard police sirens not too far away.

"Come on," the girl said. "Lee, go start the truck."

The big guy grunted and strode off toward the vehicle. The girl followed him.

"Wait," Jack said, "What if Ross comes back?"

"You mean that guy who attacked you?" the girl asked.

"Yes," Jack said, out of breath, "What… what if he comes back?"

"He won't," the girl said, "If he's smart. The police will show up in a few minutes."

"Who are you?" Jack asked trying to keep up with the girl.

They had now pushed past the ring of people and were walking down the street.

"Sarah Connors," she said, "Any more questions?"

"Any more questions?" Jack said, "I was almost shot to death!"

"Here," Sarah stopped at a large red truck that was parked on the side of the road. "Get in," she ordered.

"No way!" Jack said, "You think I'm going to just get in your truck without you telling me what happened back there?"

"Look," Sarah said, "I can't explain because it's too *complicated* for you to understand. All I can tell you is that we are here to take you and your friends to get medical help. Now please, *get in*." And with that Sarah twirled around, her blond hair flying behind her.

Jack felt himself bubbling up with anger. Too complicated? Who did Sarah think she was? But then he stopped in his tracks. Around Sarah's neck was a golden chain. And on the end of the chain was a medallion, a medallion in the shape of a triangle with an eye in the center.

"The... the mark," Jack stammered, "The mark in the book."

Sarah raised her eyebrows.

"Mark? Book?"

Jack bit his lip. Now Jack knew for sure that this girl was part of something much bigger, something to do with the book in Jacks backpack, something to do with his past, something to do with everything. He couldn't explain it, but Jack had a feeling that this girl was important. Sarah was a puzzle piece. The piece Jack was missing.

But could he really trust her? A random person he just met? On the other hand, Jack sort of had a knack for be-friending random people, even though some of those people found it amusing to try to shoot him to death. No matter how annoying Sarah might be, she could have answers.

"I need to talk to you." Jack decided. And he stumbled into the truck.

The space inside the truck was surprisingly big. Two people sat in the back seat kneeling over a third person. One of the two people was Hunter the other was the man in black. Jenifer lay on the third seat with a pillow behind her back. Jack stepped over to them.

"How… how are you?" Jack asked.

He had never actually thanked Jenifer for saving him. He owed her.

Jenifer's eyes were as foggy as a storm cloud. She blinked and looked up at him.

"Fine… I think," she managed.

There was an awkward silence.

"This is Lee Jones." Sarah said, "He's… um… well he's going to drive you to... to get help."

Lee nodded to Jack. "Well I'm not a medic, that's for sure," he said, "But I think your friend is going to be fine."

"Thanks," Jack said glancing over to Jenifer. "But why can't you just call an ambulance?"

Sarah looked behind her shoulder. "Because, well… because, like I said, it's complicated. Yes, very complicated. Lee?" Sarah said weakly, "Why don't you get in the front seat and start driving. We'll talk about it later, okay?"

"No." Jack said standing up, "How about now."

"Please," Sarah said, "Later."

Jack ignored her. "What is that?" He asked pointing to the medallion.

Sarah looked down. "Oh, what… this? It's nothing."

"Hold on a sec." Hunter exclaimed standing up, "It's that mark! The mark in the book! Jack do you see-"

"Yes," Jack said nodding, "That's it alright."

Lee and Sarah glanced nervously at each other.

"We're missing something aren't we?" Jack interrupted, "Sarah, what is it you're not telling me?"

Sarah said nothing, she just stared at Jack.

"Fine," Jack said. He pulled out the book from his bag and held it up.

"What is this?" Jack said, "And why does Ross want it?"

"Blood of the king," Sarah whispered solemnly.

Hunter and Jack exchanged bewildered looks.

"Well, that certainly clears things up," Hunter replied, nervously.

"The dollar bill," Jenifer groaned from across the truck.

Jack looked behind him and was surprised to find that Jenifer had spoken.

"The mark, Jack... the mark," she said.

Now Jack was beyond confused, he was concerned. Maybe Jenifer wasn't as well as she had let on.

"No way!" Hunter said slapping his hand to his forehead. "Why didn't I see it before? The mark is on the back of the dollar bill! No wonder Jack hasn't seen it before. He's from England!"

Jack blinked. "What?"

Hunter rolled his eyes. "You know... the green bill? On the back there's a pyramid with an eye and the little falcon dude with the olive branch?"

"Falcon dude?" Jack asked.

"It's an eagle," Sarah said looking back and forth between Jack and Hunter. "Um... Lee...we need to get back to HQ. Like right now."

Lee nodded and stepped on the gas.

"What's going on?" Jack asked. "What's HQ?"

"Just sit down," Sarah said, "You're lucky we're close. Travis wants to see you."

"Who am I?" Jack asked. He didn't know why but he felt like Sarah somehow knew the answer to that question. Sarah glanced out the window. "I'll explain everything when we get there," she said. "What is your name?"

"Jack Callow," Jack said, "And this is Hunter and Jenifer."

Sarah smiled, although it seemed a little forced. "It is nice to meet you Jack Callow.

"Same here. I think," Jack said. But really he had no idea what was going on. Clearly, this mark was special somehow. Very special...

# Jack

## The Freezing Tunnel of Sleeveless Jerks

No one spoke during the truck ride. Jack wondered if he was doing the right thing, going with Sarah and Lee. And what was up with that mark? Hunter claimed it was from the back of the dollar bill. But that didn't explain why Sarah was wearing it around her neck. And HQ? Did that stand for headquarters? Why did Ross want this book? Why was it so important?

Jack shook his head. Nothing was making sense. He was more lost than he was when he was back in England. Jack rubbed his hand against the window of the truck. The wind had picked up and it had started to rain. He wondered where they would be stopping. Suddenly, as if on cue, Lee stepped on the breaks.

They had pulled up next to a rather old, shabby looking building. The front sign read:

*F & M Antiques*

"Um… I thought this was urgent?" Hunter asked, "Why are we stopping here?"

"It is urgent." Sarah said matter-of-factly, "*Very* urgent…"

Jack stepped out of the truck and onto the wet pavement. There were no other cars anywhere. They were the only ones. He shivered. That was not a good sign, *at all.*

"So, what's the deal?" Hunter asked stepping out of the truck also. "Are we gonna go browsing for furniture or something?"

Jenifer stepped out next. Her face wasn't as pale as it was before and she was wearing a bandage on her leg, thanks to Sarah. Although she still looked very weak.

"Hunter's right," she said, "Why are we here Sarah?"

"This is headquarters." Sarah said. She started up toward the little building and Lee followed her.

Jack looked around at Hunter and Jenifer. Jenifer put a finger up to her ear and circled it, indicating, "crazy". Hunter saw the gesture and winced but said nothing. Together the three of them trudged up the pavement to the small shabby building.

The wind was blowing at them in gusts now and it was starting to sleet a lot harder. Jack didn't know what Sarah was up to, but one thing was for sure - he was missing something. Something important. He reached the building and stepped through the door way. Jack found himself in a small room filled with old books, couches, china cabinets, and pretty much everything you could think of that wasn't from the twenty first century. The place smelled exactly like it looked - damp and musty. Just another reason to make Jack even more suspicious than he already was.

Hunter and Jenifer followed him inside.

"Eeww!" Hunter said holding his hand to his nose, "What is that smell?"

Sarah and Lee were standing off to the right by a large desk. An older woman sat at the desk. She wore a black shawl and held a small green hand bag. When she spoke her voice sounded like someone was crumbling up paper.

"Sarah, how nice to see you."

Sarah nodded to the woman and looked around behind her as if to make sure no one was there. Of course no one was there, the shop was completely empty. Sarah spoke in a clear, crisp voice.

"Give me liberty, or give me death."

Jack looked up. He had heard that before, in history class, at school. It had something to do with the Revolutionary War.

The woman smiled and punched a button on her cash register, and then the weirdest thing happened. There was a clicking sound like a lock was being turned and the bookshelf to Jack's left rumbled and started to move. Jenifer leaned back in alarm as the bookshelf swung open like a door, revealing a narrow hallway.

There was stunned silence as Jack, Hunter, and Jenifer stared at the bookshelf.

"Bet you didn't see that coming," Hunter managed.

"No kidding," Jack gulped. "How did you... the bookshelf just swung..."

"Onward and upward." Sarah said briskly. She glanced at Jack. "If you are who I think you are, then we'd better get moving."

Lee grinned at Jack. "Welcome to the freezing tunnel."

"Freezing tunnel?" Jack asked, completely bewildered.

"You'll see," Lee said, "Now let's get moving. We've got to see Travis."

"Who's Travis?" Jenifer asked.

"You'll see," Lee said again, and he walked through the door... or bookshelf... or whatever!

Jack, Jenifer, and Hunter stared at each other.

"Onward and upward?" Hunter suggested.

Jack sighed, "Onward and upward."

And together the three of them plunged into the tunnel.

Ever step into a freezer? If you have, then you have a good idea of what it felt like to walk into that tunnel.

It was so cold that Jack could see ice forming on the walls.

"Who turned on the A/C?" Hunter asked as they caught up with Sarah and Lee.

"It's a cooling device that Travis installed," Sarah said proudly. "Just in case, you know, anyone got in here by accident."

"Oh, sure," Jenifer said, "I can see how *that's* necessary."

Sarah glared at Jenifer. "Keep talking like that," she said, "And you're really going to get it." And with that, Sarah strutted off down the hall like an angry peacock leaving Jenifer muttering unhappily to herself.

Jack and Hunter exchanged looks. They walked on for a few minutes longer. Hunter and Lee had struck up a conversation about baseball and were arguing about the pitching record of Mariano Rivera. Sarah walked briskly up front like she had a pole taped to her spine. And Jack tried to ignore the coldness surrounding him. He could have sworn he saw a few icicles dangling from the ceiling.

"Sorry about your leg," Jack said to Jenifer.

"It's fine," she replied.

There was an awkward silence.

"It was pretty cool the way you hit Ross over the head with your backpack," Jack offered.

Jenifer nodded, although Jack could tell she wasn't really listening.

"It's just…" she sighed, "I don't understand what's going on. Who are these people and where are they taking us? And what does this book have to do with it all?"

"If I knew the answer to that question," Jack said, "I wouldn't be here. I came to Manhattan to find out more about myself, but now I'm even more confused."

Jenifer nodded again. "Well whatever you're trying to figure out… figure it out fast, I'm freezing!"

"Right," Jack said, "No prob."

The only problem was… there was a big prob.

The tunnel continued until they reached a flight of stairs. And standing at the top of the stairs was a boy who looked maybe seventeen or eighteen. He had black hair like Jack's although his was swooped backward, fashion model style. And the moment you saw his smile you knew that this guy never forgot to brush his teeth. His eyes were a handsome brown and he wore jeans and a sleeveless tee-shirt showing off his muscular arms. Jack wondered if the guy was cold.

He wasn't doing anything, unless to consider nothing as something. But just by standing there doing nothing he managed to attract so much attention he was almost glowing. And Jack knew right off the bat that this guy was a complete jerk.

Sarah led the way up the stairs.

"That's Ethan." She said dreamily.

Hunter snorted rather loudly.

Ethan, the guy who was standing by the stairs, looked down at them.

"Well it's about time!" he said, "You guys are three days late!"

"I... um..." Sarah stammered. Her face was bright red.

"We have some new recruits," Lee interrupted. "And this one," he gestured to Jack, "Needs to see Travis."

Ethan wasn't listening at all. He was too busy flexing his arms.

"Did I mention," Lee grumbled, "That this is very urgent? I am a higher rank then you Ethan, and I have the power to take your pass!"

Jack had never seen Lee angry, and wasn't sure he wanted to. Although he could understand his frustration, having to put up with this Ethan guy could drive anyone crazy.

Ethan rolled his eyes. "Yeah, yeah, sure thing. Identification?"

Jack was expecting Lee to pull out his driver's license or something, but instead he held out a small gold coin that Jack didn't have time to see properly.

"Go on in." Ethan sighed, "Next?"

Sarah stepped forward and handed Ethan another coin. Jack was about to say that he didn't have any identification when Ethan pushed a button on the wall.

This time Jack was expecting it, so he stepped backward as the wall moved away from him on all sides. It expanded and contracted until finally there was a metal door where the wall had been.

"In you go," Lee said.

Jack put his hand on the knob of the door and was about to turn it went Ethan stopped him.

"No identification," he said smugly, "No entry."

"He's with us," Lee said through gritted teeth. And he put a hand on Jack's shoulder. Jack had to say that he was grateful for Lee. Sometimes it comes in handy to have a big strong guy with a gun on your side.

Ethan smirked at Jack. "See ya, newbie," he said. He put a hand to his fist and winked at Sarah.

"Move along," Lee said hurriedly, "No time to spare."

Sarah was too busy messing with her hair, so Lee turned the door knob and Jack, Hunter, and Jenifer peered inside.

# Hunter

Travis

Hunter was stunned. So much weird stuff had happened in the last few days. But what was through that doorway was the weirdest thing by far. Hunter couldn't even begin to describe what he saw.

The place was huge, as big as a football field! The walls were painted bright colors of green, blue, red, and yellow. Banners hung from the walls that read stuff Hunter couldn't make out. There were hundreds of small doorways, just like the one that they had come through, all along the brightly painted walls.

Hunter looked up, and right there in the middle of the ceiling was an eye just like the one from the mark in the book. And only then did he realize that the shape of this massive place was in the shape of a triangle.

People roamed about wearing pack backs and strange looking sashes like they were girl scouts. They all carried guns like Sarah and Lee, which didn't make Hunter all too excited. And he couldn't help but wonder what was in their backpacks? Maybe C4?

Jack and Jenifer stood beside him, gaping up at the place.

"This," Sarah said, "Is HQ."

"So much for antiques," Jack mumbled, still staring up at the eye.

Hunter nodded.

"First things first," Sarah said, "Jenifer, you need to get some medical attention. "Where is he..." she muttered, "Ah, here... Ryan!"

A boy who was walking past them stopped and turned around to face them. He had chocolate colored hair and a nice smile.

"Sarah, Lee," he said, "About time you guys got back. What's the problem?"

"This is Ryan," Sarah said, "One of our medics."

Ryan smiled at them.

"Nice to meet you," he said, "New recruits?"

"I guess," Hunter exclaimed, "What is this place?"

"Headquarters for the Freemasons," Ryan said as if that cleared everything up.

He must have noticed that Hunter was confused. "Don't worry," Ryan said, "We'll explain everything later. Now, how can I help?"

"We need you to take Jenifer and see if you can do anything to help her leg." Sarah exclaimed, "I'm going to take these two to Travis. And um..." Sarah gestured to Jack. Ryan raised an eyebrow.

"You think he's..."

Sarah nodded sharply. "Yes."

Hunter was starting to get scared. Ever since he had met Sarah she had acted like Jack was the most intimidating thing she could think of. Something was wrong, and he knew that Jack suspected it to.

"Let's go," Sarah said.

"Whoa, whoa, whoa!" Jenifer said, "I want to come, my leg is fine!"

Sarah and Ryan looked at each other.

"That's not the best idea," Ryan said, "Your leg doesn't look too good from what I understand."

"It's *fine*," Jenifer insisted, "It can wait until afterwards."

Ryan looked like he wanted to protest but Jenifer obviously wasn't going to back down.

"Alright," he said, "Take care you guys and um... Ernie is looking for you by the way."

"Got it," Lee said, "See you Ryan."

Ryan nodded to them and then strode off through one of the doors.

"Let's go," Sarah said again, and she walked off through another door.

Jack followed without hesitation. Jenifer nodded for Hunter to go too, and he did. Wherever Jack was going, so was Hunter. He had to make up for chickening out back at the stairs with Ethan. Hunter had wanted to help Jack, to defend him, but again just like back when they had first met Ross, all he could do was stand there tongue-tied. This time he didn't even make any comments. He was so lame. Hunter wondered why Jack even wanted him along. He was no help, just a third wheel.

Hunter thought about this as Sarah led them through doors, down crowded hallways and up flights of stairs like she had been born here. And Hunter wondered with a slight jolt if maybe she had been. What was this place, why were they here?

He had about a billon questions about this crazy building that existed underneath an antique shop. But he held back. For some reason he had a hunch that his questions were going to be answered real soon. And Hunter didn't normally follow his hunches. Usually they led him into life threatening situations, or a hot tub crowded with old people (long story.) But Hunter was sure that this was the right hunch to follow... hopefully.

They walked on and on, deeper and deeper into the maze of doors and rooms. They must have turned about twenty thousand times before Sarah finally stopped outside one of the doors.

The hallway they had come down had hardly any people in it. Hunter could tell that they were deep into the building now. The door that Sarah had stopped at had golden letters painted on it. They read:

**Travis**
**Grand Master**

Hunter glanced at Jack, but Jack wasn't looking. He was too busy reading the sign himself.

"Grand Master?" Jack asked, tentatively turning to Jenifer.

Hunter felt a slight twinge of jealousy. Jack used to turn to him when he didn't know something.

Jenifer shrugged. "I don't know what it means."

Sarah knocked on the door.

"Come in," said a voice from the room.

Hunter followed Sarah inside. The room looked like an ordinary office. It had a desk, a book shelf, and a lot of papers. Nothing out of the ordinary.

The man sitting at the desk fit right in with the room. He was wearing a work suit and tie, over-polished shoes and he held an old wooden cane. He had a neatly shaven face and his hair was short and white. His eyes were a vivid shade of green.

"You must be the ones that I was told about," he said smiling warmly. "You're all probably wondering who I am and what you're doing here."

"Yes," Jack said.

The man looked Jack square in the face. "My name is Travis," he said, "Grand Master of the Freemasons HQ 27, and we're going to have a little talk, Jack Callow."

# Hunter

## The Freemasons

Hunter sat down on a chair next to Jack and Jenifer. He knew that they were just as uneasy as he was. Hunter fiddled with the zipper on his jacket. Travis was slowly pacing up and down the room, deep in thought. Sarah and Lee stood off to the side by the door. Sarah kept on glancing nervously at Jack.

"So..." Hunter said, "Nice place you got here..."

Travis said nothing but stopped to sit at his desk. He sighed and got up again, walking back and forth. "It's true," he said, "You have the book then?"

Jack narrowed his eyes and stood up. "Alright," he said, "That is the last time I am going to have people say that and not get a straight answer! What's the deal with this book?"

Jack pulled the book out of his pack. Travis gaped at it. "Careful with that," he said desperately, "It's fragile."

Jack rolled his eyes. "I'm going to give you five seconds to explain–"

Travis put a hand on Jack's shoulder. "Sit down and I will explain everything," he promised.

Surprisingly, Jack did as he was told. He sat down waiting for an explanation. Travis looked around at all three of them.

"Do you know what the Freemasons are?" he started slowly.

"No," Jack said.

"Well, I would be surprised if you did," Travis said.

"You're a group of people that exist secretly," Hunter said unable to bare it anymore. "You exist secretly, right? And Ross said something about a headquarters. He wants this book for some reason. And so do you."

Travis exchanged looks with Sarah.

"Ross?" Travis asked.

"He's the one I talked to you about on the phone earlier," Sarah said, "The one who was attacking them."

Travis put a hand to his temple. "They have found him," he said, "They know you have the book," he continued, looking at Jack.

"Who found me," Jack said, "What's going on?"

"You don't know who you are yet, do you?" Travis asked.

"Well if everyone keeps on saying that I guess it must be true," Jack said.

Hunter noticed that Jenifer wasn't paying any attention to the conversation. She had her eyes fixed on something painted on the wall. There it was again, that mark.

As if Jenifer had been reading his thoughts she asked, "What is that, on the wall?"

Travis looked around. "That?" he asked pointing to the mark on the wall.

Jenifer nodded. "It's in the book," she added.

Jack opened the book to show Travis the page they had found in the safety deposit box.

Travis traced his hand across the mark on the page. "The All Seeing Eye," he whispered, "The symbol of the Freemasons."

"Why is it used after George Washington's name?" Hunter asked.

"Let me start from the beginning," Travis said, "The Freemasons are a group of people that exist because of one reason. Everyone who is a Freemason believes in the same thing. That every man, woman and child should be able to have life, liberty and the pursuit of happiness. Every Freemason fights for the same cause and every Freemason must be willing to give their lives for that cause. Every Mason has a mark and the mark represents that Mason. George Washington was The All Seeing Eye."

"So that's the only reason that you exist?" Jack asked, "Because you all believe in the same thing? There's got to be more than that."

"Sadly," Travis said, "There is."

"There's another group that's against you," Jenifer suggested.

Travis nodded, "You are most certainly right. There is another great power that threatens to take over this very minute. And we are doing everything that we can to stop them. But we must become stronger. And I hate to tell you this, but if you are the one I think you are, then you and the book are our only hope." He spoke to Jack as he said this. "King George's society is on the move. They have spies everywhere and it is most important that we keep you safe. It's a miracle that you made it this far. All of you."

Jack, Hunter, and Jenifer nodded, uneasily.

"There was a man at the bank," Jack started, "He said that it was best for me to be ignorant and not to know the truth. Was he…"

Travis looked at all of them. "Yes," he said, "If what you say is true, then we can guess the man at the bank was a spy for King George's Society."

"What is this other side?" Hunter asked, "What do they want with us?"

"It's not what they want *with* you," Travis explained, "It's what they want *from* you."

"They want this book and what it leads to," Jack suggested, holding up the book.

"Precisely," Travis exclaimed, "Now, I will try to tell you the full story to the best of my ability."

Everyone leaned forward and Travis began. "In the year 1760, King George the Third came to the throne of England with a plan... a secret plan. A plan of world domination." Travis looked around at Jack, Hunter and Jenifer, letting this sink in.

"And what *was* that plan?" Jack asked.

"To send colonists across to America," Travis continued, "And create a secret society of people that would one day control the entire world."

"But I thought colonists went across to America for other reasons," Hunter said. "Like better lives and religious freedom?"

"That's exactly what England wanted the rest of the world to think," Travis explained. "And many colonists did come for those reasons and had no idea what else was going on. But, King George's Society paid certain individuals, from all over, to come to America and join their society, so that they might grow stronger."

"And I'm guessing they did grow stronger," Hunter said.

"Yes," Travis replied. "Much, much stronger."

"Hold on a sec," Hunter exclaimed, "Where do the Freemasons come in to all of this?"

Travis nodded. "Good question. The Freemasons were a small group of people that broke off from the original society, and included George Washington, Thomas Jefferson, John Adams, Patrick Henry, Benjamin Franklin, and Paul Revere. They all disagreed with the Society, but weren't strong enough to stand up to them. They created their own symbols and codes so that they could communicate to one another. They made secret meeting houses and soon they had a great number of people on their side."

"But wait a minute," Jack said, "The Freemasons did rebel and so did the colonists. They won the Revolutionary War! They gained their freedom from England. Didn't this turn the tables on the Society?"

"Jack," Travis replied, "You're smart… think about it."

Jack's electric blue eyes turned to the mark on the wall. He stared at it and so did Hunter. He found himself looking right into the cold black eye.

How could this be happening? Hunter wanted to think it was a dream. But he knew that it was not. All of this was very, very real.

"It was a set-up," Jack said suddenly, "Everything was set-up."

"Exactly," Travis said. "Everything was set-up. The taxing, the Revolutionary War, Paul Reveres ride, and the Declaration of Independence. King George had planned it all out ahead of time. He wanted to create the illusion that the colonists were breaking away and forming a new independent country. This way, people would be distracted from the real plan which was to secure an entire continent and grow a culture of people who could be controlled and used for the Society's purposes."

"Why didn't the Freemasons put up a fight?" asked Hunter.

"Because King George's Society had a choke hold on the Freemasons. The Masons couldn't reveal themselves and run the risk of appearing to be against the war for freedom. They would be considered traitors. Instead, they quietly continued their meetings, slowly gaining strength and members over the years, and have never stopped working to hold back the other side," replied Travis.

"You see, the colonists who were part of the Society were actually on the side of the English, fighting a scripted war. America was never a free country. It still isn't today. The Freemasons played their parts because they were forced to. They were not nearly as strong as King George's Society. It was all planned out so that it would look as if America were a free country."

"But that means that this other society must still be in control right now, without us even realizing it," Jenifer said nervously. "How could we not have known about them?"

"They've always been in control. Our government, our schools and institutions – they're *all* working against our true freedom. Fattening us up like pigs for slaughter," Travis replied.

"What about now? Aren't the Freemasons strong enough to rise up against them?" asked Jenifer.

"The timing is crucial. We must wait until we are absolutely sure we will not lose," offered Sarah.

"Fine. This other side," Jack said, "Where are they located?"

"They're everywhere," Sarah said.

"Even if all of this is true," Hunter said, "Where does the book come into play?"

"The book," Travis said grimly, "Is the key to everything. It's a guide. And it's also the only real evidence proving that this other side exists and plans to take over. It has answers that we need. Answers that may finally help us win."

"Who wrote it?" Jenifer asked.

"The Freemasons of course," Lee said, "Who do you think?"

Travis nodded. "The Freemasons indeed," he said, "They wrote it back when they first formed, in 1761. They wrote all the details they knew about the Society's plot so that there would be a record for future Masons. After all, they were a part of it. But they knew that the Society was growing suspicious of their actions. So the Masons hid the book. And then waited, for the right time to come when they were strong enough and large enough to defeat King George's Society once and for all. At that time, they planned to release the book to the public and unveil everything.

But shortly after it was hidden, the Freemasons got word that the book was found and stolen by the other side and given to the king... King George the Third of England. The book was given to him, and then lost forever. We had assumed the book was either handed down through his decedents or destroyed. The Freemasons have been looking for the book all these years."

"And now we've found you and the book," Sarah said looking at Jack. She stared at him. "Don't you know who you are?" she said, "You're the descendent of King George - the one who started all of this. You are blood of the king. You should be working for the other side!"

Jack blinked and then shook his head. Hunter didn't know what to say. He was too shocked to do anything but just sit there pale faced. Jenifer didn't look any better. Her mouth was open and she seemed to be just as stunned as Hunter.

"Everything was set-up," Travis continued, "Including your parent's death. They knew too much. Your parents were both linguists. Apparently one of them must have descended from King George and inherited the book. We are certain they had no idea what the book contained. They were simply intrigued by its contents, we assume, and they were trying to figure out the meaning of the book. But their actions raised suspicion and the Society became aware of their research. They were murdered. They never died in a car crash. They were murdered by King George's Society."

Hunter looked at Jack and could almost feel his pain.

Travis continued on, "But your parents were obviously smart because they made sure that the book stayed with you. They never knew about the Freemasons or anything else but they did know that the book was somehow very important. They knew they were being followed, so they placed you and some of their belongings with another family, far enough away to be out of danger, thinking it would be only temporary. Your parents may not have understood everything, they may not have even known what they were facing, but they were brave and they tried to do the right thing for you," Travis finished.

"How... how do you know all of this about me?" Jack asked.

"The Freemasons been watching over you," Sarah said, "To protect you."

"And we were hoping that you were in possession of the book," Travis added. "The moment you got on that cargo ship, everything exploded into chaos. King George's Society has been following you, watching your every move. As have we."

"That must be why Ross found us in Nova Scotia. He was waiting for us," Jack said.

"And we've been waiting for a chance to intercept you," Lee added.

"They're growing too strong," Travis put in, "They know that Jack has the book and they will do everything in their power to get it from him."

"Where does the book lead to?" Jenifer asked, "They must want it for some reason."

"What do you mean, *'lead to'*?" Travis asked, "The book contains all the secret information. It doesn't lead anywhere."

"But there isn't any information. The book is blank." Hunter said, "All we have is this single page that Jack found in the safety deposit box."

"Actually we have a little more than that," Jack said, as he flipped to the back of the book. "I didn't show this to you earlier because I haven't been able to figure out what it means yet," he added, looking at Hunter and Jenifer. "It looks like some sort of code. Travis, is this what you meant by the book being a guide?" he asked.

"What? How can the book be blank?" Travis asked, shocked.

Jack leaned forward and showed Travis the book up close. Every page was blank except for the one with the handwritten series of marks Jack had tried to decipher and the page Jack had retrieved from the box at the bank.

"Where did this come from? This isn't the Freemasons book," Travis said, confused.

"It's got to be, because this page I found in the box with the mark on it fits into the book perfectly," Jack explained, showing Travis.

"Jack, how come you never showed us the markings on the last page?" Jenifer asked, sounding hurt.

Hunter nodded in agreement. "Yeah, Dude. I thought you trusted us?"

Meanwhile Travis, Sarah and Lee were all huddled around the book, examining the page of markings. "Hold on a second. This is one of the codes of the Freemasons," Travis said.

"Yes, I recognize it too. It's very old. Not used much anymore," Sarah added.

"You mean the last page?" asked Jack. "Is that a language?"

"Sort of," Travis trailed off, now sitting down examining the code in further depth.

"Guys, I'm sorry I didn't show you the markings," Jack said to Hunter and Jenifer. "Our situation was already too complicated. I didn't want to make it worse," he added.

Hunter knew that Jack was holding something back. They had sat for hours talking with him about the book. He had plenty of time to bring up the markings. Hunter had a feeling it must have been because Jack didn't want to admit he couldn't figure it out.

"Give me that page you found in the box," Travis ordered. Jack handed over the page and Travis examined it next to the page with the Freemason's code. Finally, he stepped back and stared at Jack. "I don't know how this can be possible," Travis began.

"But I think that we're dealing with a mystery bigger than we realized. It's true, this is not the original book."

"Well, what is it, then?" asked Hunter.

"It appears that this book at one time contained pages of clues," Travis explained. He read from the code he had just deciphered, "Travel the path the riddles reveal to seek the book that has been concealed."

"So, where are the clues now?" Jack asked.

"Well, it's obvious, isn't it? Someone has hidden the clues," Hunter chimed in. "We have the first one, the one your parents put in the safety deposit box, which probably leads to the next one," he concluded.

"But the other side must know about the clues too. They're also looking for them!" Jenifer said.

"We have to remember one thing," Travis said, "We have the advantage. The clues were left by the Freemasons so that means that we are more familiar with them than King George's Society."

Jack nodded in agreement.

"We know where the next page is," Hunter said abruptly, "It's in Rome, The Colosseum."

Travis stared at him, surprised.

Jack stood up alarmed. "Oh no!" he said, "Ross knows. He knows where the next page is. He overheard us talking!"

"What?" Sarah said, "Why didn't you tell me?"

"In all the commotion I forgot!" Jack said desperately, "He's probably on his way to Rome right now!"

"Well, we need to get there first," Hunter said.

"Yes, and get the clues to find the book, just like the code explained," Jenifer said, standing up.

"Yes" Travis said, "We're the only thing that stands in the way of King George's Society taking over and covering up what they have done. We must secure the book. It is the only proof of their existence."

Hunter sighed, "So we have to save the world without the world knowing that we saved the world."

"Exactly," Travis nodded. "And one more thing. I'm sorry to say that you three must stay put. We need you safe."

"No!" Jack protested. "We're going. Together."

"Yes!" Jenifer said standing up as well, "All three of us are going!"

"It's too dangerous," Travis said, "I can't have three inexperienced teenagers wandering around-"

"I'll take them," Sarah said abruptly.

No one spoke. Hunter felt dizzy. Sarah go with them?

"You'll need someone with experience," she said smartly, "I've been around the world. I can be your guide."

Hunter knew that none of them were too enthusiastic about having Sarah along, but no one argued. Not even Jack. Travis nodded his approval and looked around at all of them. "We'd better get going then," he said, "I'm afraid that our enemy is on the move."

# Hunter

## Departure

Hunter walked out of Travis's office in a daze. Everything he had heard in there was... well... crazy. It pained him to even think about it, but it was the truth.

Sarah led them back through the maze of rooms until she stopped at one of the doors.

"You two may sleep in here," she said to Jack and Hunter, "Jenifer you're coming with me to see Ryan."

Sarah turned on her heel and walked back toward the direction of Travis's office.

"Sarah," Jack said awkwardly, "Thanks."

She gave him a quizzical look. "For what?" she asked.

"For volunteering to go with us," Jack said.

She nodded slowly like she wasn't sure if he was joking or not. "You're welcome," she said finally, and then walked stiffly away.

Hunter looked at Jack but said nothing. They both said good bye to Jenifer and stepped into their assigned room. Hunter was relieved to find beds, a bathroom and even a little mini fridge.

"This is awesome!" Hunter said excitedly, all of his doubts fading away.

Both boys found clean clothes on the beds, including jeans, white t-shirts and black jackets. Hunter figured Sarah must have phoned ahead to say that they would be coming.

He took a shower, changed, and ate a bag of chips (which were free!) Hunter was feeling better than he had in long time. Jack looked better too. His black hair wasn't full of dirt anymore.

"Better than Jenifer's place, right?" Hunter said enthusiastically as they both slipped into their beds.

Jack nodded. He hadn't spoken since their visit to Travis. Hunter tried to understand the way he felt. It was a lot to take in all at once.

Hunter lay in his bed and thought of home… Chicago. He had come so far. His old life seemed like a fantasy. And now he was going out to save the world? Funny the way things happen so fast. The only thing Hunter wasn't sure about was Sarah. She was so stubborn and so annoying at times. Would she slow them down? Yes, she was experienced and older then all of them (but only by a year.) Someone should have spoken up and said something against it. But no one had said anything. And strangely, Jack had seemed perfectly happy about having Sarah along. What was up with that?

Hunter rolled over and his thoughts drifted into dreams. He wasn't sure how long he had slept before Jack was shaking him awake.

"Hunter," he said, "Wake up. Sarah's here. And she's taking us to the training place. She said something about proper gear."

Hunter blinked the sleep out of his eyes and then stumbled out of bed. The room was filled with light from a lamp that had been turned on in the corner. Hunter dressed and had some breakfast of eggs, bacon, and pancakes which had been laid out on the table for him.

"How did the food get here?" he asked Jack as he sat down next to him.

Jack shrugged. "It was here when I woke up," he said taking a bite of pancake.

"How can you eat that?" Hunter asked looking down at his pancake, "It's burnt!"

Jack smiled. "That's just the way I like it," he said taking another bite. "Now let's hurry. Jenifer's already out there."

Hunter found that Jack was right as he opened the door of their room. Jenifer was standing next to Sarah and Ryan. Her leg was still bandaged, but she seemed to be moving around more easily.

"Wow," Jack said in surprise, "You look better."

Jenifer nodded. "It wasn't that bad," she said, "The bullet just grazed my leg. I didn't even need stitches."

Hunter shook his head. "You are one lucky dumpster girl."

Jenifer laughed. "You bet."

"We'd better get going," Sarah said, "Onward and upward."

Jenifer made a face, and they all followed Sarah back down the hall.

By the time they had gotten to the "training area" Hunter was starting to feel nervous. They walked through a set of big double doors and into a massive room filled with all sorts of equipment. He hoped he wouldn't have to fight anyone. Not that he couldn't... it's just he wasn't wearing the right shoes.

"Nice," Jack said as they walked around.

But apparently Sarah didn't have any reason to stop because she kept on walking, through the room and another set of doors. Hunter stepped through and found himself looking at every type of gadget you could imagine. There were walkie-talkies, guns, backpacks, explosives, knives, and multiple flat screen TV's.

"Wow!" Hunter said in amazement.

Sarah walked casually through the room handing items to Jack, Hunter, and Jenifer.

"You'll need this," she said handing them all walkie-talkies, "And a gun always comes in handy."

After they had all been given their supplies, Sarah led them back to Travis's office. They said good bye to Ryan and then the door was shut.

"Now..." Travis said slowly looking around at them all, "Once you find the next page of the book or anything at all, come back here immediately. We'll need to figure it out together. Here are your tickets."

He handed them each an airline ticket.

"Any questions?" Travis asked.

"Yes," Hunter said, pointing to his gear "How is this stuff supposed to get through the metal detector?"

Travis's eye's twinkled mischievously.

"I've made arrangements for that," he said, "Now get going. Lee is driving you to the airport. Once there, I'm afraid you're on your own. Remember... the world depends on you."

"Yeah," Lee said, just entering the room, "But no pressure."

"Sure," Jack gulped.

"And one last thing before you go. You'll need this," Travis said.

He handed Jack a wallet filled with money.

"Right," Jack said taking the wallet a little awkwardly.

Hunter whistled. "I get some of that, right?" he asked.

Jack slipped the wallet into his pocket and nodded to Hunter. "Later," he said, "First let's get on the plane. I've got a feeling that it's going to be a lot more comfortable than a cargo ship."

# Hunter

## Rome

Hunter sat in his seat on the plane. They were just about to take off. Jack sat on one side of him and Jenifer sat on the other. Sarah sat in the aisle in front of them reading a magazine.

Hunter was sure that they would be caught when they had gone through the metal detector with all of their weapons. But just as Travis had said, he had made arrangements. The man who was working there had let them pass after he had seen Sarah's coin. Hunter was grateful they had gotten on so easily.

Just then, Jenifer tapped him. "So how high do we go?" she asked nervously.

Hunter raised his eyebrows. "You've never been on an airplane before?" he said.

It was only after he said it that he realized how stupid it sounded. Of course Jenifer had never been on a plane before. "Pretty high," Hunter said recovering himself, "Normally above the clouds," and he smiled.

Jenifer sat back and gripped her armrests tightly. "That's pretty high," she said.

"So this is what I was thinking," Jack said leaning over to show Hunter a napkin he had been drawing on.

On the napkin were a bunch of symbols.

"What are they?" Hunter asked.

Jack held up a dollar bill he had pulled out of the wallet. "They're various symbols that were used by the Freemasons," he said, "Sarah was telling me on the way over here. I was copying them off of these bills so I could look at them more closely. Sarah thinks that the next page of the book will be marked in some way by one of these symbols."

Hunter looked more closely and found that he recognized one of them. It was the eagle from the dollar bill. He had to admit that Jack was a pretty good artist. Of course Hunter was good too… sort of.

Suddenly the plane started to move onto the run way.

"How fast do we go?" Jack asked looking out the window.

"Wait a second," Hunter said looking back and forth between Jack and Jenifer, "I'm the only one who has been on a plane before? So that means that I've done something that neither one of you have done before?"

"Yes, Hunter," Jenifer said irritably, "Congratulations."

Hunter nodded, satisfied and slumped back down in his seat. "As long as you two admit it," he said, "Now, are you going to eat that bag of pretzels or what?"

The rest of the flight was spent looking over the symbols and discussing where they were going to start. Sarah tried to talk with them, but finally the guy she was sitting next to got kind of angry when she turned around to say something and knocked her drink into his lap. After that they decided to give up and just rest for the remainder of the flight.

When they finally landed at their destination, Sarah said that they were just outside of Rome. All they had to do now was rent a car and drive to the Colosseum. Hunter thought that everything was going pretty smoothly.

They rented a car at the airport with some of the money Travis had given them. Hunter wasn't sure if the Italians were on to something or just plain stupid. Instead of making bigger parking spots they made their cars the size of go-carts. Hunter, Jack, and Jenifer were squeezed into the back seat of a compact car. That and the fact that Sarah was a terrible driver were just about enough to make Hunter go… yes, crazy. Sarah drove like a maniac and Hunter was surprised he hadn't thrown up by the time they got into Rome.

A short time later, Sarah came to a halt in front of the Colosseum, just around dusk. It towered over them like a gigantic soup bowl with a crack in it. Hunter wondered whether or not they would be able to find the mark they were looking for in this gigantic place.

Sarah interrupted his thoughts. "We have another half an hour before we can enter," she said.

"Why?" asked Jenifer. "There are plenty of people going in now, and it must be closing soon."

"Because Travis said entry would be arranged after hours," replied Sarah curtly.

Now Hunter wasn't sure what was going on. He glanced at Jack, who seemed equally confused.

"So, what do we do now?" Hunter asked.

"We wait," said Sarah simply.

Hunter pulled out an apple from his backpack and munched on it nervously. He saw that Jack was pulling out the napkin with the symbols he had been working on in the airplane. Nearly an hour passed as the group waited and watched tourists depart. It was getting cooler and darker now.

Hunter was anxious to just get going and get inside the Colosseum. He was tired of examining documents and looking at symbols. "What exactly are we waiting for?" Hunter asked no one in particular.

"Safe entry. Another Mason," said Sarah.

"How long is this gonna take?" shot back Hunter.

"Listen, if you want to get in alive, and locate this symbol, you need to be patient," Sarah responded, looking around, annoyed, as if expecting something or someone.

"Who are we waiting for?" asked Jack.

Just then, a security guard approached them. They were the only people left, lingering near the entry.

"Oh, great," thought Hunter. He wanted to punch Sarah for making them wait and now making them targets. "We'll probably get arrested before we even get started," he thought, angrily.

The guard approached Sarah and Hunter felt like he recognized the guy from somewhere but he didn't know where. He had on glasses so it was hard to tell. "Cold, isn't it?" the guard asked Sarah politely.

"Yes, but the eagle is warm," she answered.

"Huh?" thought Hunter. What is it with this girl?

"Follow me," the guard stated, and turned back toward the Colosseum.

The guard walked them around the side of the Colosseum and to a small back entrance that didn't seem to get much use. It was very dark and difficult to see where he was walking. He heard someone stumble and curse, but he couldn't see who lost their footing.

Jack had pulled a flashlight out of his bag and was attempting to look around when the guard grabbed his arm and warned sternly, "Put that away! Follow my orders precisely!"

Jack nodded, nervously, and continued shuffling along the inside wall of the entryway.

Hunter followed Jack through the darkness trailing his hand along the rock. Suddenly the rock ended and Hunter lost his footing. He bumped into someone.

"Ouch!" Jenifer screamed jumping in the air.

"Quiet," Sarah scolded from Hunters right.

Hunter could just make out the dim outline of his friends standing around him.

"Where are we?" Jack whispered.

There was no reply and Hunter was starting to worry that no one knew where they were.

"Just keep moving,' the guard said finally.

Hunter did as he was told. He followed the others across the slippery rock floor until finally he stepped out into the starlight. Hunter could see everyone clearly now. He looked behind him and realized that they had come out of a stone passageway and into the Colosseum. Only, someone was missing.

"Where's Sarah?" Jenifer asked, "She was right behind me a second ago."

"Maybe she got lost?" Hunter said hopefully.

"I don't think so," Jack figured.

"It's possible she got lost in the passages," the guard said. "This is not good. You three." He nodded to them. "I sense something is wrong. Stick together until I return and don't use your lights."

And with that, he walked off back the way they had come.

"Great," Jack said "Now what are we supposed to do?"

"Have a look around?" Jenifer suggested.

"Or, we could run away from that figure that's coming at us," Hunter added backing away into another passage to their left.

# Hunter

## Christians and Crosses

Hunter managed to pull out his gun although he didn't think he had what it took to shoot anyone.

"Who's there?" Jack asked fumbling with his flash light.

"Cool it," came a voice, "It's me. And Hunter, put that down! Someone could see you!"

Sarah hurried toward them looking flustered. Hunter felt a mixture of relief and disappointment.

"Where were you?" Jenifer asked, "That guard just left us here."

"Nothing," Sarah said quickly, "I just got lost, that's all. Those passageways are dark."

Hunter noticed a gash on her arm like someone had taken a knife to her. Sarah must have seen him looking at it because she covered it up with her sleeve.

"I tripped," she said nervously glancing behind her, "Hit my arm on a rock."

"Right," Hunter said, "I assume you probably tripped again after that and that's why you're limping."

"Don't be an idiot," Sarah hissed, "We need to focus on finding the mark. What would be the most obvious place to look?"

"What about the guard?" Hunter asked, "He said we should wait here."

"We need to focus on finding the mark," Sarah repeated.

"Let's move into the center of the arena," said Jack, "and try to get our bearings. After that we can split up."

The others agreed, although Hunter wasn't sure about splitting up. But of course they did move into the arena and they did split up.

Hunter and Jack walked around the inside of the seating. There were bleacher style seats that had been built over the top of some of the original stone. It also looked as though the structure had been braced with metal bars in some areas.

Hunter didn't know exactly what they were looking for, but he kept his eyes open for anything peculiar that might catch his attention.

Suddenly, Jack stopped. "I'm so stupid," he said, "I should have thought of this before." He pointed up toward the narrower side of the arena to a large platform in which a metal cross stood. "That must be the north side of the arena," said Jack.

"How do you know?" asked Hunter.

"Because that's where the Imperial Box is located," replied Jack. "It's where the emperor sat during the gladiator tournaments. It would be one of the most obvious places to put the mark because it's one of the most important places in the Colosseum."

"Let's go check it out," said Hunter.

Jack pulled out his flashlight and Hunter said, "The guard told you not to be using that."

"Well, I'm sick of guards. And besides, Sarah's not exactly following the rules herself. Where do you suppose she was?" asked Jack.

"I don't know," said Hunter, "But I'm pretty sure she didn't get lost. Something's up."

They approached the cross. Hunter walked slowly, as if something were about to occur.

Jack shined his light around the base of the cross. It was smooth and shiny with no obvious marks. "This is wrong," said Jack, "The emperor's seat is missing. See." Jack shined his light around the platform as well. Up close, it was easy to see that the platform was put in recently. A placard next to the cross explained that the Imperial Box once stood in this location but had been moved to be restored. The cross was placed in this spot to remember the Christians who died there. It also said something about the ground being unstable but Hunter wasn't in the mood to read about support systems.

"Well great!" he said, "There's no box. Now what do we do? It doesn't say where the box was moved to."

Jack stamped his foot in frustration. "There's got to be something here!"

"Let's try somewhere else," Hunter suggested, "Maybe the girls have found something. This place is huge!"

Jack ignored Hunter and stepped up onto the platform for a better look. Jack bent down and felt the cross with his hand.

"It's so smooth," he said "no sign of a mark."

"Come on Jack," Hunter insisted, "There's nothing here."

Jack started pacing back and forth on the platform. Hunter was getting annoyed now.

"Christians," Jack mumbled, "Christians."

"What?" Hunter asked.

"What do Christians do?" Jack said suddenly.

"What are you talking about?" Hunter exclaimed.

"What do Christians do?" Jack repeated.

"I don't know." Hunter said, taken aback, "They worship God I guess."

Jack smiled. "Exactly!" he said.

"Are you all right?" Hunter asked nervously.

"We thought we were looking for a specific sign," Jack said excitedly.

"Yeah..." Hunter said.

"The cross *is* the sign!" Jack exclaimed. "Christians trust in God!"

Hunter's eye's widened. "In God We Trust." he said.

"Yes!" Jack said, "In God We Trust is a clue. It's referring to the Christians. And what is the mark of the Christians?"

"The cross!" Hunter said with triumph. "And that must mean that the Freemasons put the cross here on purpose. Not to remember the Christians who died here. The cross was put here because *it's* the actual clue!"

Jack nodded. "Come on!"

# Jenifer

## The Scary Dark Hole

Jenifer wasn't happy. Why did she have to get stuck with Sarah? She hoped that the boys had found something so that she could get out of these creepy ruins. Jenifer could have sworn she had seen something move.

Jenifer and Sarah had been walking along some of the stone ruins when Sarah stopped in her tracks.

"What is it?" Jenifer asked suddenly getting a chill up her spine.

"Thought I heard something," Sarah mumbled.

Jenifer couldn't help but notice that Sarah was acting rather odd. Ever since Sarah had gotten lost she had seemed like she was anticipating something.

"Oh! Shut up." Jenifer told herself, "You're making yourself jumpy."

She had noticed that there were placards here and there, although it was too dark to read them without a flashlight.

"This is pointless!" Jenifer said out loud, "How the heck are we supposed to find this page if we can't see anything?"

But before Sarah had time to answer, a light started flashing from the other side of the Colosseum.

"Are they mad?" Sarah hissed. "We'll all get caught!"

"Better go see what it's all about," Jenifer said, already starting to jog back the way they had come.

As both girls got closer they saw that Jack and Hunter were both heaving a metal cross down from a platform. Their flash light was on and Jack was trying desperately to manage the cross and at the same time shine the light on where they were walking. It wasn't working so well.

Jenifer ran forward and helped to steady the cross. The three of them got down off the platform and laid the cross down on the ground.

"Geez," Hunter said, "I didn't think it would weigh that much!"

"What are you doing?" Sarah said tensely, "We have to get out of here, now!"

"Aren't you the one who got us in here?" Jenifer asked.

"Look," Jack said interrupting the argument, "This cross is the mark. We have to find out what it means."

Jenifer knelt down and studied the cross.

"How are you sure?" Jenifer asked.

"I'm sure," Jack said simply.

"Hey guys! You guys might want to see this." Hunter said.

He was standing back up on the platform and was peering down at something.

They all ran over to him and found that Hunter was standing at the top of a hole.

"Whoa!" Jack said shining his light on it. "How could we not have seen that?"

"It was dark," Hunter said, "I guess the cross must have been on top of it."

"Well, it's deep," Jenifer said, "What do you think is down there?"

"There's only one way to find out," Jack said, "Sarah? What is it?"

Sarah was staring behind her like she was expecting something. "Nothing," she said, "Thought I saw something."

Jack and Jenifer exchanged looks.

"So," Hunter said, "Who wants to go down the scary dark hole first?"

Descending the hole was easy. It was plenty big enough for a person to fit through. Sarah was picked to go through first since she had the most experience.

Jack tied her up with a harness and rope from his backpack and Sarah was lowered into the hole. She climbed down rock climber style, letting herself fall down backwards very slowly, keeping her feet on the wall at all times.

"Anything down there?" Hunter called into the darkness.

"I think I hit the bottom!" a voice called from the pit, "It looks like there's another passage down here."

"We're coming down," Jack called back.

"We are?" Jenifer asked, looking down at the hole with displeasure.

"This may be our only chance," Jack said, "Jenifer when you come down tie the rope around those rocks so we can get back up."

"I'm going last?" Jenifer asked.

But Jack was already descending into the pit.

As Jenifer climbed down the wall she though she saw movement at the edge of the hole. She remembered what the guard had said: "I sense something is wrong."

"Oh, shut up," Jenifer told herself.

She reached the bottom with a thud and found the others standing around her. Jenifer noticed that the bottom of the pit snaked off in two directions creating a passage.

"Which way do we go?" Jenifer asked dusting herself off.

Jack shone his light across the walls. There were paintings of men with swords and nets. There were images of men killing wild animals and other men.

"This way," Jack said suddenly.

"How do you know?" Hunter asked him.

"Look." Jack pointed to the wall. On the wall was a very detailed painting of a cross. Next to the cross was a painting of the eagle from the back of the dollar bill. Jenifer figured that each symbol marked a passage.

"Another cross," Jenifer said.

"Why should we follow the cross?" Sarah asked, "The eagle would be more likely to follow. It's a well-known symbol of the Freemasons."

"I'm guessing that they're trying to trick us," Hunter said, "The cross marked the place where this passage was. They want to make sure that we really discovered the secret and we didn't just get in here by accident."

Jenifer hadn't thought about it that way and she was surprised that Hunter was the one to figure it out.

"So then, we'll follow the cross," Jack said.

Sarah looked like she wanted to ague but probably realized that they were right.

# Jenifer

## Guess What? More Holes!

They had been following the stone passageway for only a short while before they came to a fork in the road. But this time it was not hard to choose which passageway to take. All they had to do was follow the cross.

They followed the cross for a long time until the passageway started to get wider on both sides and then they were standing in a small room. Jenifer could barely see anything even with the light of her flashlight.

"Where are we?" She asked.

"Oh no," Hunter groaned. "We hit a dead end."

Jenifer felt the walls around her and found that Hunter was right. All she could feel around her was cold stone wall. There was nothing in the room at all.

"I told you," Sarah said, "We never should have come down here!"

"Aren't you the one who volunteered to come on this trip with us," Jenifer shot back. "We don't want you anyway! I want to know what you were doing when we went through that passage. You didn't really get lost!"

"Stop!" Jack yelled, "Stop both of you! We'll never get anywhere by arguing!"

Jenifer knew that he was right but she still felt like arguing.

"I think I found something!" Hunter shouted from over to Jenifer's right, "Oh no," he said reluctantly, "I just tripped over my backpack."

"Uhg! There's got to be something here!" Sarah said angrily stamping her foot on the ground.

There was a loud creaking noise and Sarah yelped, jumping backward into Jack.

"Watch it!" Jack said.

Jenifer bent down and felt the ground where Sarah had been standing. The ground seemed to have collapsed in on itself. No! It was a trap door!

"Jack!" Jenifer said excitedly, "I found something."

Jack bent down next to her. "Wow!" He said, "It's... it's..."

"A trap door!" Hunter said, "But more importantly it means that I was right!"

"Sarah you must have opened it with your foot," Jenifer said.

"And look at this," Jack said excitedly. He shone his flashlight onto the trap door. The image of the cross was engraved in the wood. Jack kicked the door the rest of the way open and peered down into the hole. "There's a ladder," he announced, "Should we head down?"

The last thing that Jenifer wanted to do was to climb down another dark hole, but she followed Jack down anyway.

As they climbed further down the ladder Jenifer noticed patterns on the walls. No, not patterns. Symbols.

Jenifer's feet touched the ground at last and she found herself in another room. Jack stood next to her on the ground.

"Aww! Come on man!" Hunter said stepping down after Jenifer, "No more rooms."

"We are here!" Jack said finally stepping forward and pointing to the symbol that was painted on the back stone wall. "The All Seeing Eye."

Bellow the triangular mark there was a stone table and on the table laid a small gold box. Just a box.

# Jenifer

## The Next Page

Everyone advanced slowly toward the box, not making a sound. Jack blew away the dust and lifted the lid. It seemed as if the whole room was holding its breath. Well at least Jenifer was.

Jenifer strained her eyes to see what was in the box. Another clue? Jack lifted a piece of old yellow paper up and out of the box. He grinned.

"The next page!" he said.

"What's it say?" Hunter asked excitedly.

Jack held the paper in the light of his flashlight beam and read:

*Within the celestial hall resting above the seat of power, four characters bring forth good will.*

*Jefferson* 

Jenifer sighed. "Another riddle," she said, "I don't suppose that you know this one too. Do you Jack?"

"Maybe Jefferson has something to do with it." Hunter said helpfully, "After all he's the one who signed it."

Jack pulled the book out of his back pack and fit the page into it.

"Come on," he said, "We can discuss this back at the car. Personally I would like to get out of this ditch."

"No kidding," Hunter mumbled.

The four of them climbed back up through the trap door and shined their lights around the walls looking for the exit.

"Looking for something?" came a voice from behind them.

Jenifer whirled around to find a figure standing by the exit. The person advanced, his green eyes shining.

"Why hello Jenifer!" Ross said happily, "How's your leg? Get it all fixed up?"

Jenifer was tongue tied. "How dare you!" she managed.

Ross chuckled. "And I see that you brought little Miss Sarah along for the trip as well! Lovely! Now where is the page? I know you found it! Give it to me!"

"Never!" Jack said.

"Ah, Jack," Ross said with fake sarcasm, "You think you can find a clue and save the world? It doesn't work that way. Don't listen to anything that white haired phony tells you. Join us! We have bigger plans than just toying with stupid kids. Once we have this book... you have no idea!"

"I'll never join you!" Jack shouted.

"Well then," Ross said holding up his gun, "I guess I have no choice."

"No!" Sarah said, "Please!"

"Too late!" Ross bellowed.

"You're right," came another voice from somewhere behind Ross, "You are too late."

Ross whirled around and standing behind him with his gun out was the guard... but it wasn't the guard. He had taken of his hat and glasses. And that's when Jenifer realized.

"Lee!" Jenifer shouted, feeling relief flood over her.

They were saved.

# Jenifer

## The Guard Again

Ross looked back and forth between Lee and Sarah.

"I was in town so I decided to stop by," Lee said with a smile. "Is everyone okay?"

"Fine," Hunter said.

Jenifer looked at Ross and realized that his expression of surprise had shifted to anger.

"We were in the middle of a very important talk. Do you mind coming back later?" Ross said. "Now give me the book!"

"First tell me what you were going to say," Jack insisted, "You said you have bigger plans?"

"Oh yes," Ross said, "This book is only the beginning! Now give it to me!"

"Don't!" Lee shouted, "I'll shoot you Ross!"

"If you shoot me," Ross said, "I'll shoot the boy."

"You want the book?" Jack shouted, "You can have the book."

"Jack," Sarah warned, "What are you…"

Jack kicked open the trapdoor and chucked the book down the hole.

"No!" Jenifer said staring at the hole, "Why–"

"Come on!" Jack yelled and he sprinted from the room.

"Ha ha!" Ross said, "He values his own life more than the world! The fool!"

Lee fired a shot at Ross but he was too late. Ross was already gone down the ladder and had closed the door behind him.

"Come on!" Jack shouted again.

They had no choice. All four of them ran after Jack through the winding maze of crosses.

# Jenifer

## Dreams

Jenifer grabbed hold of the rope and pulled herself up. Her friends stood around her on the platform in the Colosseum. The sun was rising, sending streaks of red and gold into the heavens.

A single cry was heard from the hole, "JACK CALLOW!" Jack and Hunter moved the cross back over the hole and retrieved the rope.

"What have you done?" Lee said. He almost sounded angry.

"You lost the book!" Sarah said, "Do you have any idea-"

"It's okay," Jack explained, "When we were coming up the ladder from the room where we found the page, I heard something above us... so I..." He held up three neatly torn pages. Jenifer could just make out that they were the two clues and the page of markings from the back of the book. "Just as a precaution," Jack said as everyone sighed with relief.

"You are truly something special," Lee said shaking his head, "And that reminds me. Travis wishes for you to return to Manhattan for as long as it takes for you to figure out the next clue."

"But I don't understand something," Hunter said, "How did you find us."

"Later," Lee said, "I think we should get out of here before someone sees us or…" Lee jerked his head toward the cross, "Oh yeah, and by the way, that tunnel doesn't have any back exits does it?"

"No," Jack said as they started to walk toward the car, "Everything was blocked off."

Jenifer was only half listening to the conversation. Her mind was wandering back to her life on the streets. She had changed so much in such a short time. She suddenly realized that she was exhausted and could barely walk. It had been such a long night and they hadn't gotten any sleep at all!

They all squeezed into the tiny car and that is when Jenifer fell asleep for good. She dreamed of her new friends and of their success, and everything that lay ahead. Everything good.

# Jack

## Old Friends and New Beginnings

They arrived at the antique shop the next day and Jack couldn't have been happier to see the moving book cases or the freezing tunnel or even Ethan.

They walked through the door and the entire underground building erupted into applause. Jack found himself being patted on the back by people he didn't even know. Ryan waved to them from the crowd.

"Well done!" voices shouted. "You got the page!" shouted others.

Jack had never been more embarrassed, excited, terrified, and overwhelmed in his entire life.

When the fuss finally settled down and Jack and his friends were allowed some breathing room, Travis stepped forward and announced, "Welcome fellow Masons! I present to you three of our newest recruits. They willingly volunteered for a mission not all of us could have done. They showed that they are strong, and loyal. So therefore I recommend them for Entered Apprentices!"

Sarah must have seen their look of confusion because she muttered, "You have to get recommend by at least three higher degrees in order to move up. Entered Apprentice is the First Degree."

Jack nodded.

"I recommend them as well," Lee said.

Sarah nodded her agreement along with many others.

"Then it's settled!" Travis boomed. "Welcome fellow Masons!"

"Welcome fellow Masons!" everyone repeated.

Jack was swept away with the crowd to the dining hall. Well, at least Jack assumed that it was the dining hall. It was big and had tables set up in rows of thirteen (Jack counted them.)

The rest of the night was a total blur. Jack sat down at a table with his friends where they were served a huge assortment of food. Many of the Masons stood up and made toasts in their honor. Jack found the whole night very overwhelming but at the same time he felt at home. He enjoyed chatting with his new friends.

"So everyone here has a degree?" Jack asked Lee after they were served.

"Yeah," Lee replied, "Everyone here does. And we all have jobs as well."

"Jobs?" Hunter asked, "What do you mean jobs?"

"You get to choose what type of job you want," Lee explained, "There are guards and scouts and medics, you name it. Of course you won't have to worry about that until you get your next degree."

"What degree are you?" Jack asked.

"Sarah I and are both 5th degrees. Perfect Masters."

Sarah beamed with pride. "We know all of the secret passwords and we are allowed to go to the classified part of the library, where all the confidential documents are located."

Jack nodded and then turned to Hunter and Jenifer, his two best friends who had volunteered to come with him even though they knew the risks. And Jack wondered about himself. He had found what he had set out to find but now he almost wished he were back home. The word home sounded so welcoming that it was hard to resist.

When their dinner was finished and everyone had become quiet, Travis stood before them and made his announcements. He had no microphone or speakers but his voice seemed to carry throughout the whole room, reaching every corner of the hall.

"We have introduced to you three of our newest Masons. But as we all know every Mason has a mark. So therefore I have prepared for our three new friends coins with their own marks. These marks will be their new symbols. New marks on history."

Everyone applauded as Jack, Hunter and Jenifer were forced out of their seats and up to the front of the hall. Travis handed Jenifer a small golden coin with a symbol etched into the metal. Jack couldn't make it out but before he could say anything Travis announced, "The Olive Branch!"

Next Travis moved to Hunter and handed him another golden coin. "The Square and the Compass!"

Travis moved to Jack last. Jack could feel his heart thumping. What would he get? Travis placed the last coin into Jacks hand winking at Jack as he did so. Jack looked down at his coin and smiled. "The All Seeing Eye!"

Everyone applauded them for the last time as the three friends went and sat back down. The cheer sounded triumphant. And Jack felt triumphant as he took his seat.

"We're in this together." Jack said.

Hunter smiled. "Totally," he said in French.

Jenifer smiled as well. "You can count on me."

Everyone looked at Sarah. "Well," she said, "if you guys don't want me to come then-"

"You're our guide, we need you," Jenifer said.

"Yeah," Hunter said, "Besides, it's good to have someone along who is more annoying than I am."

"Yes," Jack agreed, "We need you. You're the only person out of the four of us who really knows what they're doing."

Sarah slowly nodded, "I guess I'll come."

"We need like a team name," Hunter said, "I was thinking, 'The Hunter is Awesome' team. Pretty good, right? Really gets your attention."

"I know," Jack said, "The Seekers of the Clues."

Jenifer nodded her approval. "I like it."

"Well then" Jack exclaimed, "It's settled. We are The Seekers of the Clues!"

That night after dinner, Jack and Hunter headed to their room. Jenifer said good night to them and slipped into the room across from them. It had been decided that tomorrow the three of them would start their training as Freemasons and begin to decipher the next clue. The only problem was that Jack could not stop thinking about home. He wanted to see his parents again. He had found what he needed to know and now he wanted to go back. Jack wasn't sure what to do.

Travis held Jack up at the door of his room. "Jack," he said, "You don't need to do this, you know."

Jack stared at him. "What do you mean?" he asked.

"I made you and your friends Freemasons for a reason." Travis said looking right into Jack's eyes. "Do you know what that reason is?"

Jack thought for a moment. "Because you knew that I was the one you had been waiting for, the one who would defeat the other side?"

"Precisely," Travis exclaimed, "I knew from the moment I saw you that you were the one. I wasn't so sure about Hunter and Jenifer but they have proven themselves to me. And I have confidence that all three of you will make good Masons and most importantly, a good team."

Jack slowly nodded.

"But," Travis continued, "You do not have to continue on this path. I know that you long to go home. And I feel bad about putting all of this into your hands. I want you to know that you do not need to stay."

Jack stared at him completely stunned. "You're giving me a choice?"

Travis smiled. "We have the next clue now. There is no reason to put you through anymore."

Jack couldn't believe what he was hearing. "But didn't you just say that I was the one?"

"You are," Travis replied very simply. "But you must choose your own path. Stay or go?"

Jack had the opportunity to go home! He could just leave and never have to worry about any of this anymore. But Jack knew what he had to do. He knew deep down that he could never leave.

"I think I'll stay," he stated.

"And why is that?" Travis asked.

Jack hesitated. "Because I can't leave my friends," he decided.

"Well put," Travis replied, smiling wide. "I am glad to have you on our side. This is something we must fight together. Alone we would not stand a chance."

"Thank you," Jack said, "And can I ask you something?"

"Certainly," Travis said.

"Why did you give me The All Seeing Eye?"

Travis thought for a moment. "The All Seeing Eye is a symbol of power and bravery. But most importantly, it is a symbol of leadership. And you are a leader Jack and a good one. You are braver than you think. And I know that you will always be there for your friends, no matter what happens."

Jack took out the gold coin and studied it in his hand. The symbol of the eye looked ancient and powerful.

"Carry this coin with pride. You are The All Seeing Eye," Travis said, laying a hand on Jack's shoulder.

Jack lay in his bed that night and thought about his talk with Travis. He could have gone home. But he had chosen the hard road. And one thing was clear to Jack now. He knew who he was and that he had done the right thing in coming to Manhattan. He was a Freemason now and it was his duty to find the rest of these clues. Jack and his friends.

Jack realized he was ready to contact his parents. He wanted them to know he was safe. He sat up in bed and pulled his journal out of his pack. He hadn't written in it since he'd left home. He tore out a page and began to write.

*Dear Mum and Dad,*

*I want you to know that I am alright and that you shouldn't worry.*

Jack stopped writing. He wasn't sure what else to say. It wasn't like he could just openly tell his parents everything that had happened. He thought about what else he could say. Jack couldn't tell his parents where he was, or they would come looking for him. And he couldn't tell them where he had been because they wouldn't believe him. So that only left him with one option. He continued writing.

*I am safe and have found good friends that are protecting me. They always have been. I miss home and want more than anything to return, but I have matters to deal with that I believe will keep me busy for a while. I am extremely sorry for any pain that I may have caused you in my disappearance. I don't know what lies ahead of me in the future but I do know that I am happy now. When I have finished what I have to do, I will write to you again. I hope I will see you sooner than I predict.*

Jack stopped again. What more was there to say? *Thank you for being my parents.*

*Love, Jack*

He was tempted to put his new mark after his signature, like George Washington had, but he knew it was pointless. What would that mean to Jack's parents?

Suddenly a horrible thought crept into Jacks mind. Ross... Jack had completely forgotten about Ross. Had he escaped? Or was he still stuck down in that underground passage? These questions swam in Jacks mind until he finally got up and headed for the door. He was about to open it when there was a slight knock. Jack opened the door and found Jenifer standing there.

"Can I come in?" she asked, "I need to talk to you about something."

Jack nodded his agreement and stepped aside for her to enter. "I just got up to come and find you actually," Jack whispered.

"I'll wake up Hunter," Jenifer replied.

After a few minutes they all sat together on the floor.

"Have you looked at your coins?" Jenifer asked the two boys.

They both nodded. "What do you think these symbols mean?" Hunter asked.

"Well, Travis told me after dinner that the symbols can mean something different for each person unless two people are very similar," Jenifer said.

"He told you that?" Jack asked.

"Yes," Jenifer said, "So that means you must be a lot like George Washington! But I came to tell you something else as well." Jenifer suddenly sounded very serious. "I think that Ross has escaped."

The room was silent for a few seconds.

"I was thinking the same thing," Hunter said. "I have this feeling."

Jack nodded. "Me too, that's why I was coming to find you Jenifer."

"But if Ross has escaped," Hunter asked, "Then that means we'd better get trained and prepared for what's coming."

Jack looked at both of his friends. They had been through so much together.  And now it was time for the next part of their mission… seeking the clues.

# Symbols of the Freemasons

## The All Seeing Eye

The All Seeing Eye is one of the most well known marks of the Freemasons. The eye seen on the top of the pyramid is supposedly a recreation of the "Eye of Horus" in ancient Egyptian religion. It has also been known as "The Evil Eye" or "The Eye of God."

"Annuit Cœptis" and "Novus Ordo Seclorum" are the words written around the pyramid. In English this means: "Providence favors our undertakings" and "New world order." These mottos were suggested by Charles Thomson. On June 20, 1782, Congress approved, and this Latin phrase was printed on the dollar bill.

At the base of the pyramid the roman numerals MDCCLXXVI stand out to the naked eye. Decoded, these numerals mean: 1776. 1776 was the date that the Declaration of Independence was signed.

**Annuit Cœptis**

**Novus Ordo Seclorum**

**MDCCLXXVI**

The All Seeing Eye will always be a mystery and some argue that it is worthless to even attempt to try and decode it. While others say that they are just beginning to understand what it all means. No one may ever know what these marks mean or what they are for, but one thing is for sure. They were left here for a reason.

**The Eagle**

The Eagle is another very well known symbol. As we all know the Eagle is the symbol of the United States of America and of freedom. That is the exact reason that the eagle was chosen for the dollar bill, it reminded the states of their freedom.

The coat of arms that is seen on the eagle's chest is used by the United States Government, on letterheads, numerous departmental seals of the United States Government, and even license plates.

The shield the coat of arms is on has two obvious differences from the American flag. First there are no stars at all on the blue side of the seal, and second; the outer most strips are white instead of red.

The shield is held by the bald eagle which is holding thirteen arrows in its left talon (referring to the thirteen states) and an olive branch in its right. This proves that America has a great desire for peace but is also always ready for war. The olive branch has thirteen leaves and thirteen olives (again referring to the thirteen states.)

The eagle itself has exactly 65 feathers, which in gematria is the value of the Hebrew phrase YAM YAWCHOD (together in unity.)

**Degrees**

The Freemasons had 6 basic degrees. When you became a Freemason you started as an *Entered Apprentice*. From then on you had to be recommended by another person in a higher degree in order to move up. This made it a huge accomplishment for anyone to become a Grand Master.

1st degree: Entered Apprentice

2nd degree: Fellow Craft

3rd degree: Master Mason

4th degree: secret Master

5th degree: Perfect Master

6th degree: Grand Master

## Famous Freemasons

Benjamin Franklin (1706-1790)

Frederick the Great (1712-1786)

George Washington (1732-1799)

Franz Haydn (1732 -1809)

John Adams (1735-1826)

Paul Revere (1735-1818)

John Hancock (1737-1793)

Tomas Jefferson (1743-1826)

Johann Wolfgang von Goethe (1749-1832)

Wolfgang Amadeus Mozart (1756-1791)

Robert Burns (1759-1796)

Ludwig Van Beethoven (1770-1827)

Henry Ford (1863-1947)

Winston Churchill (1874-1965)

Harry Houdini (1874-1926)

Cecil B. Demille (1881-1959)

**Sir Alexander Fleming** (1881-1955)

**Franklin Delano Roosevelt** (1882-1945)

**Douglas Fairbanks Sr.** (1883-1939)

**Irving Berlin** (1888-1989)

**Oliver Hardy** (1892-1957)

**Duke Ellington** (1899-1974)

**Clark Gable** (1901-1960)

**Charles Lindbergh** (1902-1974)

**William "Court" Basie** (1904-1984)

**Gene Autry** (1907-1998)

**Gerald Ford** (1913-2006)

**Nat "King" Cole** (1919-1965)

**Travis Jefferson** (1943-present)

**Lee Jones** (1956- present)

**Sarah Connors** (1994- present)

**Ryan Adams** (1995- present)

**Ethan Parry** (1995- present)

**Jack Callow** (1996- present)

**Jenifer Bright** (1996- present)

**Hunter Truman** (1997- present)

## About The Author

This is Charles Besjak's first novel. He is a twelve year old homeschooling student who lives with his family in Watchung, New Jersey. He enjoys reading historical fiction and adventure novels. This novel is the first in the series *The Seekers of the Clues.*

Made in United States
Orlando, FL
17 April 2022

16938028R00117